THE THIRD SON

S. E. GREEN

PART I

Carter

1

 dim light illuminates the hotel suite.

Outside storm clouds move in. Thunder rumbles.

A red-haired woman moves toward me, her naked body cast in shadows.

I down the rest of my beer.

She smiles. I smile.

In two swallows she drinks the vodka she took from the mini bar.

I'm drunk. She's drunk.

Laughing, she falls on top of me. The tiny vodka bottle rolls across the comforter.

We kiss.

Reaching down, she grasps me.

I enter her in one thrust...

With a jerk, I snap awake. The ceiling spins, and I squeeze my eyes shut, breathing deeply. When next I look, the ceiling's stopped spinning and I sit up.

My wife, Tori, lays beside me asleep. On her night stand a sound machine fills the room with trickling Zen-like water.

She stirs, and her voice comes raspy from sleep, "Carter, you okay?"

"Yeah, just a dream." I slide back under the sheets and winter comforter.

Tori snuggles into my side and I automatically open my arm, so she can lay her head on my chest. My fingers glide through her thin straight hair to massage her scalp. "Go back to sleep," I whisper.

With a deep breath, she melts into my body seconds away from being in REM.

My eyes stay wide as I stare at the unmoving ceiling fan in the center of the room.

That night in the hotel happened over a decade ago with a woman whose name I never knew.

Why would I be remembering her now?

2

The next morning, I stand cooking at our island range. My five-year-old stepson Nathan sits on a padded bar stool glaring at the scrambled eggs that I just placed in front of him. "They're runny."

"They're not runny."

His incredulous brown eyes scroll from his plate up to me.

"Fine, they're runny. What's it going to take, kid?"

"A Hawaiian bread roll to sop it up."

"I'll see you a roll and raise you five bites of cantaloupe."

He ponders the wager. "Deal."

I unwrap the bread, tear off a roll, and hand it to him. He wedges his index finger down and circles it around, making a large hole. With his fork, he shovels the two scrambled eggs in and pats them down.

Then with a goofy and toothless grin, he takes a big bite. "Mmmm. Mmmm. Mmmm."

"Way to key up the drama." From the refrigerator, I get the Tupperware of already cut cantaloupe and put five little chunks on his plate.

Tori comes down the stairs dressed in white wool slacks with a red-fitted tucked-in top. She stops at the floor-to-ceiling windows that look out over the ridge and Tennessee hills that roll right to the Smoky Mountains. A light dusting of January snow glows in the clear morning sun.

With a dreamy sigh, she turns away. "I love our home."

"Me too." From the mug caddy in the corner, I take her favorite pink one with green lettering scripted *Dear Mom, At least you don't have ugly children* and I fill it with French Press coffee.

Her sensible heels click on the hard wood floor as she crosses the great room that makes up our entire downstairs. She stops at the rustic framed mirror and finger combs her dark bangs. "Are we sure we're liking the new cut?"

"We're sure."

With a smile, she turns away and inhales. "Please tell me I smell bacon."

"Yep." I hand her the mug.

"Dude, I told you she was scoping you out." Daniel, my 12-year-old stepson, jogs down the steps. "Did you look at her Insta?" He laughs. "Did you see that shot of her in a bikini?"

"Daniel," Tori calmly speaks. "Hang up, please."

Dressed in jeans and an orange hoodie, he rounds the landing. "I know!" He bypasses the amazing view that Tori just took in and flings himself onto the L-shaped tan leather couch that faces the stone fireplace. He laughs.

"Daniel," Tori speaks again. "Hang up."

He holds a finger in the air and keeps right on talking.

Tori and Nathan look at me with matching do-something brown eyes.

I hand the spatula off to Tori and in my socks, I tread over to Daniel. I don't ask. I simply take the phone from his fingers, say, "He'll see you at school," and I hang up.

"Carter, what the—"

"Watch your language." I wave the phone in the air. "You get it back when you leave for school. Now, come eat breakfast like a civilized human. We want to talk to you and your brother."

~

FIVE MINUTES later Daniel sits on a bar stool next to his younger brother shoveling eggs in his mouth. Well, if there's one thing I can say about the boy, Hawaiian bread roll or not, he never complains my eggs are runny.

Tori places her Mom mug on the speckled granite island. She looks between her boys before nervously glancing my way. It always amazes me how she can argue a case in court and debate any topic with finesse and keen intellect, but when it comes to her sons, anxious energy drives her.

I'd like to think that'll be different once we make things official with them. She'll feel more settled. Maybe the boys will, too. I know I will.

She clears her throat. "We've been married a year now and living here as a family. I think it's been going well. Do you?"

"I do!" Nathan enthusiastically looks at Daniel who crams an entire piece of buttered wheat toast in his mouth.

"Daniel?" Tori prompts.

He shrugs.

Her burgundy tinted lips press together. I step closer, not touching her, but letting her feel my warmth and support. She wanted to be the one in charge this morning, so I let her take things at her pace.

"Carter loves you two very much," she says.

"I do," I agree.

"We'd like to officially make him your father. He'd like to adopt you."

Nathan's little face scrunches up. "I don't get it. I thought he was already our dad."

"No, stupid. Our dad's dead." Daniel spears a chunk of cantaloupe and eats it. "Why do you think we call him Carter?"

Tori points a finger. "Do not call your brother stupid."

Daniel chews the cantaloupe with a little too much force. He doesn't look at me or Tori. He looks at his plate that's almost empty.

One piece of fruit left and he'll have nothing left to fiddle with. He jabs that piece with his fork and eats it.

Tori runs an uneasy finger back and forth across the rim of her coffee mug. She stares at the crown of Daniel's dark head, waiting I think for him to finish. Finally, he does, letting his fork clank loudly as he slides his plate away. If Tori thought he'd make eye contact after eating, she's mistaken. Instead, he folds his arms and stares at a crumb laying on the granite where his plate was.

I might be wrong, but I think I catch a glimpse of tears in his eyes.

"As a stepparent, Carter doesn't have legal jurisdiction to make decisions for you two. He can't officially give consent to your medical care. He can't sign school forms. He can't even pick you up from school without my approval. Once he has custody, he'll be able to do all those things and more."

Nathan's mouth puckers into a frown. He looks over at Daniel. Daniel stares at that crumb.

I look at Tori. *Do you mind?*

She waves me on.

I love her beyond words, but she tends to fall back on work jargon when she's anxious. "Nathan, Daniel, I want you to know how much I loved your dad. We were best friends. We did everything together, going back to college. I was so sad when he died. I cried hard. You lost your father, and I lost my best friend." I wave my arm around the kitchen. "Did you know I helped him design this house? He was so excited to build this for you two boys. The two of you meant the entire world to him." I laugh. "Gosh, he was so excited when you were born. I don't ever want to replace him. I could *never* replace him. John was one of a kind. But, I want you to know I love being in your life. Right now, I'm permanently in your mom's life because we're married. I'd love to permanently be in yours too by adopting you."

"Do I have to call you Dad?" Daniel quietly asks.

I'd love nothing more. "Not unless you want to. No pressure."

Nathan squirms in his seat. He'd call me Daddy today if Daniel would approve.

I wink at Nathan before looking back at Daniel. "We won't do it unless all four of us are on board, okay? Take some time and think about it."

Finally, Daniel lifts his head. "What about my last name?"

Tori says, "We'd like to hyphenate it, so you'll have both Carter's last name and your dad's. You'll be Daniel Grady-Lambert."

"And I'll be Nathan Grady-Lambert?"

We nod.

"Are you two going to make a baby?" Nathan asks.

That question punches into me, but I focus on composure. As much as the baby topic affects me, it touches Tori on another whole level.

A sad smile creases her face. "We would love to make a baby together, but I can't anymore."

I do touch her now, running a slow hand down her spine. She leans into me, accepting the comforting gesture.

"Okay." Daniel slides off the kitchen stool to stand. "I guess I'm on board."

Nathan grins. "Me, too!"

3

After dropping the boys at the bus stop, I navigate my Jeep Renegade back up the steep ridge to our home and park between two stilts.

Inside, I slide the heat to 68 from the 72 that the family prefers. I'm the only one home during the day, so what I feel goes.

My boots I place on the bottom shelf of the shoe rack. My thick flannel I loop on the wall-mounted brass hooks. In my socks, I cross over the great room to the far corner where my home office sits.

Secured to the drafting table are blueprints to a home I've been commissioned to design on Lookout Mountain. Split level with three bedrooms and three bathrooms, it'll have floor-to-ceiling windows like our home with mountain views from every room.

I wish John was still alive. He'd be proud of this design.

Back in the kitchen, I refresh my coffee, then settle at my desk to start my day.

Fifteen minutes into returning emails, Tori texts me, I THINK THAT WENT WELL.

ME TOO, I text back.

WE'LL SIGN THE PAPERWORK THIS WEEKEND?

I give her a thumbs-up emoji, then, STIR FRY FOR DINNER?

She gives me a thumbs-up emoji as a call comes in.

GOTTA TAKE A CALL, I quickly text before answering. "Hello?"

"Yes, this is Dr. Porter calling from Murfreesboro Medical Center. Is this Carter Grady?"

"It is."

"I'm sorry to inform you that Rachelle Meade suffered an accident and died."

A beat goes by. "I'm sorry, who?"

"Rachelle Meade."

"I don't know anybody named Rachelle Meade."

"Not according to her medical records. You are listed as next of kin."

"That's impossible." I put my phone on speaker and type, "Rachelle Meade, Murfreesboro," into a search engine. A link pops up to a local seamstress. From there I pull up a photo of a red-haired woman.

Shit. "Um, yeah, okay. I just looked her up. I know her. We're not related, though."

"Not to her, no. But to her ten-year-old son, you are."

~

"I HAVE to go to Murfreesboro on business," I tell Tori that night as we're getting ready for bed.

She finishes writing in her red leather journal before setting it aside. "When?"

"Tomorrow."

"That seems sudden."

"Mm, yeah." I walk over to the gun cabinet and flick on the interior night light. "I'm meeting with a prospective client. Should be back home tomorrow night."

"Okay, I'll handle stuff with the boys." With that, she goes to the bathroom, closing the door. I slide into bed and under the comforter.

Rolling on my side, I give the bathroom door my back, and I stare at the white hand-knotted throw rug peeking out beneath our bed.

I barely remember that night with Rachelle Meade. I'd been in the Murfreesboro area at a conference. It was the last night and a bunch of us went to the bar. I lost track of how many beers I drank, of how many martinis I bought Rachelle. The inebriated night ended in my room.

When I woke up in the morning she was already gone.

The first thing I did was check my wallet. She'd taken twenty dollars in cash, but that was it.

The second thing I did was schedule an exam to make sure I didn't catch an STD.

The third thing I did was block the whole encounter from my mind. Last night's dream was the first time I'd thought of it in years.

Sure, I've had one-night stands but never without a condom and never as drunk as I was that night.

Rachelle Meade and a possible ten-year-old son.

What the hell am I going to do?

4

———

I'm up before the sun. Tori doesn't even stir as I kiss her goodbye.

It takes me almost five hours to go from East Tennessee to Murfreesboro via Monteagle Mountain which thankfully isn't closed due to ice.

I'm waiting outside the hospital's mortuary when the hour turns to nine.

A tall gray-haired man wearing work boots, overalls, and a beat-up black leather jacket rounds the corner. He comes to a hesitant stop when he sees me. "Carter Grady?"

I stand. "Yes."

"You're here earlier than I thought." He approaches, extending a large hand. "I'm Dr. Porter. Sorry about the attire. My son usually feeds our cows, but he's on a school trip to D.C. this week."

"That's fine." I shake his hand, finding it smoother than expected.

He unlocks a glass-paneled door, and I follow him into a small office. Filing cabinets line the left side, a steel desk takes up the right side, and a closed door along the back leads into what I assume is his work room. Beside that door, a hook holds a white lab coat.

After sliding out of his leather jacket, he sits, motioning me to do the same. "Make yourself comfortable."

Folders and loose papers scatter his desk. A framed photo shows a teenage boy in braces grinning for his school picture. A large flat-screen monitor displays a dancing snowman screen saver.

Oddly, the space smells like vanilla. I expected something more sterile like bleach.

He motions behind him and to the right where a mini-fridge sits. "Can I get you water or green tea? I don't drink coffee."

"No, thank you." Nerves move through my stomach and I take a slow breath.

"I'll need you to identify the body. Then you'll take the paternity test. From there it will be a few days to get the results."

"The boy. What is his name? Where is he right now?"

"A local family is fostering him. I'm not permitted to give you his name. That will be at social services discretion."

"You said Rachelle was in an accident?"

"Carbon Monoxide poisoning. She fell asleep with a gas-powered space heater on. The flame went out, but the gas kept coming. She died in her sleep. The boy found her the next morning and called nine-one-one."

"How is it he survived?"

"His window was open, and his door was closed. The space heater was in Rachelle's bedroom." He looks across his desk, lifting folders and putting them back down until he finds the one that he wants. "Have you ever identified a body before?"

"No."

"It's very different than what you see on TV. I won't be leading you into the morgue and pulling the body from a freezer. I'll be showing you a photograph right here at this desk. Take your time with it. There's no one here rushing you. You won't see a picture of her whole body, just her face. We know who she is already, but this is a formality." He looks at me for a second. "It's natural to be nervous."

I glance down to the folder he's holding, feeling my anxiety ease a bit. I only have to look at her photo. "Okay, I'm ready."

He slides out an eight-by-ten colored picture of Rachelle Meade's face and bare shoulders. She looks like she did on the website, but her eyes are closed like she's sleeping, and her lips are slightly blue. Her red hair lays combed back from her face and tucked under her shoulders, indicating it's long.

I have a quick flash of her laughing all those years ago, flirting with me as I flirted right back. Later, rolling around in bed, going at it as only two uninhibited drunk people could. Why didn't she contact me when she found out she was pregnant? She obviously knew my name.

I hand the photo back. "We had a one-night stand eleven years ago. From what I can remember, yes, that is her."

5

From Dr. Porter's office, I take the elevator upstairs where he said a social worker would be waiting for me at the lab.

Young with dark curly hair and olive-toned skin, a woman dressed in a jean skirt, boots, and a thick cream sweater stands leaning up against the wall as she scrolls her phone. On the floor beside her sits a cross-body bag with a red wool coat folded on top.

"Joanie White?" I approach.

She glances up, offering a big bright grin. "Good morning. I take it you're Carter Grady?"

With a nod, I extend my hand, and we shake in greeting.

She looks like she's right out of college.

She points to the closed door. A plaque on the wall beside it reads LAB. "This is where you'll do the paternity test. It's just a cheek swab. I'll wait here. When you're done, we'll find a private place to chat."

∾

THIRTY MINUTES later we sit across from each other at a corner table in the hospital cafeteria. Being between breakfast and lunch it's an odd hour and we have the place practically to ourselves.

From the grease scent clinging in the air, I suspect they're prepping fried chicken for lunch.

We each have coffee. She offered to buy me something to eat, but I declined. I'm too anxious for food. I probably should have passed on the coffee as well.

"It'll take three to five days to get the results of the test," she says. "In the meantime, let's talk through a few things."

"Okay."

"As far as we can tell, you are the only relative to Francis Meade. Rachelle—"

"Francis? That's his name?"

"Yes." She smiles, giving me a second with that monumental yet tiny nugget of information.

Francis Meade. What a cute name.

"Rachelle has no family that we've been able to locate. If the paternity test comes back positive, know that you have options. You can sign over rights and he'll become a ward of the state. He'll enter the foster system and be eligible for adoption."

My nerves ratchet up. I've known about Francis only since yesterday morning, but I can't imagine I'll sign over anything.

"If you choose to exercise your parental rights, we'll work in conjunction with social services in your home county to make the transition go as smooth as possible."

Leaving my coffee untouched, I sit back in my chair and close my eyes. My brain spins with about a zillion things, but the three names it whirls through on repeat are Tori, Daniel, Nathan.

Tori, Daniel, Nathan.

Tori, Daniel, Nathan.

"I know this is a lot," the social worker calmly speaks.

"I got married last year. I'm in the process of adopting her two sons." I open my eyes back up. "What am I going to do?"

"Have you talked to your wife?"

"No, I didn't want to until I knew for sure."

"I understand."

"Am I allowed to meet Francis?"

"Not until the test comes back. But I can show you a picture."

My heart kicks in, and I sit back up. "Okay."

She opens the flap of her canvas bag and extracts a white folder.

"When was he born?" I ask.

"August fifth."

"That's consistent with our one-night stand," I say more to myself than her.

I expect to see a posed school picture but instead, she hands me a five-by-seven photo. "I took that yesterday."

A blonde hair boy stands with his back to a wall painted deep blue. It makes his matching eyes jump from the photo. Blonde hair and blue eyes, just like me.

"He's small for his age," she says.

"So was I."

His lips hold a small smile, but his eyes don't.

"What grade is he in? Fifth?"

"He's been home schooled his whole life. We don't have accurate records yet."

I don't stop staring at the photo of my son because even though I don't have the test results I know in my gut that he's just that —my son.

My son.

He's wearing a buttoned-up shirt and bowtie with his hair neatly combed in a side part. He looks like a tiny professor. "Did you make him wear that tie?"

"No. He wanted to."

"Can you tell me anything? What does he like? Where did he grow up? Is he a meat-eater or vegan? Does he play baseball? Because I was a baseball player. Does he like video games?"

She smiles. "I don't know. He lived isolated out in the country in a trailer. The home was clean and stocked with groceries. There was no TV, but lots of books, puzzles, and wooden toys. Rachelle rented. She didn't own. She was a seamstress. The nearest neighbor lived miles away. No one really knew her. I ran Francis through all the usual questions we ask in these situations."

"Like?"

"When was the last time you ate? When was the last time you had a bath? Does your Mom leave you alone? Do you have any injuries?" She keeps rattling off questions, and I can barely keep up. She stops talking. "I can email you the list if you'd like?"

"Yes, thank you."

"I will say, in the small amount of time we've interacted he comes across like a polite and well-adjusted young man."

"Polite or not, that sounds like a sad way to grow up."

Her smile becomes tight, and I detect something else. I hand the photo back. "What aren't you telling me?"

She hesitates, clearly unsure if she should say more. "Let's focus on getting the results back."

6

Francis Meade, my ten-year-old son.

My brain won't quite wrap around that.

As far back as I can remember, I've wanted a family. I envied those friends who had it. I admonished those who screwed it up. I've never been the type to go from woman to woman. I'm a serial monogamist. I like commitment. I work well in a relationship. I'm devoted. I'm all in. I'm ready to build a life.

I've simply been unlucky in love.

Then, John Lambert, my best friend and colleague died, leaving a wife, an eight-year-old, and a one-year-old alone. I was already an "uncle" to the boys and a friend to the family. I didn't hesitate to help Tori with anything she needed. They say you find love when you stop looking. I suppose that's what happened with the two of us. Our friendship gradually turned to more. Now here I am at forty-five with the wife and kids I've always dreamt of.

If you would have told me that I'd one day be married to my best friend's wife, I'd have laughed it off.

I'm happy. I really am. But if I had to pick one thing that I wish I had, it would be a biological child. I'd never say that to Tori, though. It would crush her. Though I suspect she knows it.

What is she going to think about all of this? She's got a big heart. She'll welcome him into our lives. Or at least I think she will. She wouldn't give an ultimatum—it's her and the boys, or Francis —would she?

No, of course not.

"'Morning," she murmurs, nuzzling into me and bringing me from my thoughts. "How'd it go yesterday?"

"Good."

Her mouth travels along my neck as she slides a leg over my lap to straddle me. My wife loves morning sex. My hands slide along her bare thighs and up and under her oversized tee. She moves against my growing erection and closing my eyes, I suppress a grin.

She giggles. "Is this one of those mornings where I do all the work?"

"I did have a long day yesterday," I tease.

Her hand finds its way inside my pajama bottoms, and she strokes me. "Then just lay there. This won't take long."

~

THIRTY MINUTES later I'm standing in the kitchen at the island range cooking breakfast and idly listening to Nathan ramble about teaching his guinea pig, M&M, a trick. I highly doubt he taught the guinea pig anything. It's the laziest damn pet I've ever seen.

Daniel sits beside his brother and as usual, he's on his phone. Normally, I'd remind him to put it down during breakfast, but I'm not in the mood to tackle that battle right now.

Joanie, the social worker, said it would be three to five days to get the results back. I should've thought to ask if I could pay to put a rush on it. I'll call in a little while after everyone is gone.

I also want to look at Rachelle Meade's website again. Maybe she's got a social link to Facebook. Who knows, I might come across pictures of Francis. Come to think of it, I could hire a private investi-gator to track down more details. Joanie didn't seem to know a whole lot about Rachelle's extended family.

"Carter!" Daniel waves a hand in front of my face.

It's then I notice the sausage is smoking. "Sorry." I turn the flame off and slide the skillet away.

Daniel peeks at the burnt meat. "I'll still eat it."

"Runny eggs. Burnt sausage." Nathan crinkles his nose. "You're not too good at the cooking thing."

True. But at least I try.

Breakfast comes and goes. They go upstairs to brush their teeth before school. Tori comes down, ready for work. It's all so normal. I hate that I'm about to upset everything.

She sniffs the air. "What'd you burn?"

"Sausage. I smothered it in maple syrup. They ate it anyway."

Laughing, she hands me a green folder. "That's the petition for adoption. Just sign and then we'll appear in front of a judge to finalize."

I turn away, wiping a counter I've already wiped. "Okay, I'll look over it and sign it later."

"Oh... do you want me to put it in your office?"

"Sure, thanks." I listen to her heels tap against the wood floor as she crosses the great room and into my office. I hate this.

When she comes back, I put the rag in the sink and face her straight on. Confusion moves through her big expressive brown eyes. The boys barrel back downstairs, veering off to the side door. While they zip into their jackets, Tori quietly studies me. She knows something's off.

7

I wish I had a business trip that would keep me away for a few days. Luckily my wife is working late tonight. When she gets home, I'll pretend like I'm asleep. I won't have to see her until tomorrow morning.

By then, hopefully, I'll know what to say.

I spend the first hour searching for more information on Rachelle Meade, but I get nowhere. Other than the website I initially saw, it's like she doesn't exist. I try to remember anything from that night we had our one-night stand and form vague impressions at best. There was a cute red-haired woman, a lot of drinking, laughing, falling onto the bed...I barely remember the sex, and I certainly can't recall anything we talked about.

Hell, I didn't even know her name until Dr. Porter said it.

A brief call to Joanie White confirms I'll have to wait patiently for the results. Putting a rush on things isn't going to happen.

I'm about to start researching private investigators when my calendar dings reminding me of a meeting.

That meeting leads to another. A deadline gets moved up. A new contract comes in. A client isn't happy. Another conference call. I'm digging through zoning laws when the phone chimes that I have to pick the boys up from school.

From there it's football conditioning for Daniel, gymnastics for Nathan, then home for showers, dinner, homework, and finally bed.

I don't have to pretend to be asleep when Tori finally walks in.

In the morning, she rolls out of bed and goes straight into the bathroom. There is no morning snuggle. No tender *'Morning.* Not even eye contact.

Normally I would do my thing in the bathroom, then head straight down to start breakfast, but this morning I stay in bed and I wait.

The shower kicks on, followed by the exhaust fan. Quietly, I listen.

Minutes later the water goes off.

Minutes after that, the door opens. With a towel around her head and a thick white robe tied around her body, Tori steps from the bathroom. She stops when she sees me sitting in bed.

"Good morning," I say.

"'Morning." She walks into the closet and comes out with a gray skirt and a black cashmere sweater. She lays both on the bed. "I checked your office when I got home last night. Why haven't you signed the papers?"

A knock comes on our door. "Mommy?" Nathan says. "Carter? I'm hungry."

"Give me a few minutes, Buddy," I call out. "You can have TV time while you wait on me."

"Okay."

I listen to the sound of his feet shuffling away.

"Have you changed your mind?" Tori calmly asks in her lawyerly tone.

"No." I take a breath. "But we need to talk."

Tori doesn't move.

"What are your thoughts on a third child?"

She hesitates, clearly taken off guard. "You know I can't have another baby."

"I know. But what about adoption?"

She moves then, finally coming over to sit on the bed. But she takes the corner farthest away from me as possible. "I mean, I guess I'd be open to another. But I'd like to wait a few years. We just got married, you're about to adopt the boys, I think it's too soon to throw yet another thing into their lives."

Crap. That isn't what I wanted to hear.

Another knock comes on our door. "Mom? Carter? Nathan's bugging me to make him breakfast."

"Jesus Christ," she mumbles, pushing off the bed. She charges over to the door, pauses, then patiently opens it. "Good morning, Daniel. Carter and I are talking. Why don't you be a fabulous brother and go make Nathan a bowl of cereal?"

"Fine," he grumbles.

She closes the door and comes back over to the bed. This time she sits right beside me and takes my hand. "What's going on?"

God, I love this woman. I'm just going to say it. Like ripping off a band-aid. "I might have a ten-year-old son."

8

Tori processes things in a quiet contemplative way. She doesn't like to talk until she's ready. It's the one thing John complained about to me, and I get it now. I'm a talker, just like John was. I like to get it out there, deal with it, then move on.

Understandably, Tori is in shock. I'm not sure if I should've waited until I knew the results were positive. Who knows in these situations? I had to trust my gut. She knew something was going on. Putting it off would've caused even more tension between us.

So, when she didn't respond to my bomb of a statement, it didn't surprise me. She went to work. I took the boys to school. And now here I am in my office.

I'M GOING TO VISIT THEIR GRAVES AT 6, she texts me around lunch.

She only visits the graves on the anniversary of their deaths, or when she's in deep thought.

I text back, MEET YOU THERE?

YES.

Her response brings me relief. She's not completely shutting me out.

Thankfully, work jams the rest of my day, and I'm left with little time for my own thoughts.

The boys have nothing after school, so they ride the bus home. They're both doing homework when I hear Tori's SUV park under the house. A moment later, I catch sight of her walking away from the house and down the valley. She traded her dress shoes for galoshes.

After sliding into my boots, I tread the valley down to where she waits. The setting sun clings to the horizon, casting the mountain peaks in vibrant hues of orange that soften as they roll into the valleys. The air is clear and cold with not a hint of wind.

As I come to a stop beside her, I glance over my shoulder back up the snow-covered hill to our home. Every once in a while, I'll look out of the house and see Daniel sitting here next to his dad's grave. He's never said it, but I think he likes to come down here and talk to his dad about stuff that's on his mind. Someday I hope he'll talk to me about those things.

Nathan only comes down here when either Tori or I am with him. Except he doesn't talk to his dad, he talks to his twin sister, Samantha.

Samantha lived to be an hour old. She was in an unusual position that caused a lack of oxygen flow. Tori's hemorrhaging during labor led to an emergency hysterectomy. She's never told me any of this, but John did. He said Tori never even got to hold her daughter. I've tried a few times to talk to her about it, but she cuts me off every time. She never discusses Samantha.

Instead, she writes her thoughts in a journal that I never read. She leaves it on her bedside table. I've been tempted many times to look inside, but I never do. Like with Daniel, I hope Tori will one day talk to me about it.

They're a lot alike that way—Daniel and Tori.

In her arms, she holds two bouquets of flowers—one full of wild-flowers and one with lilies. She hands them to me before taking a soft-bristled brush from her jacket pocket. She tends to John's memorial stone first, carefully cleaning the snow off the grass-level, gray and black granite.

JOHN LYNN LAMBERT
GONE TOO SOON

When she's done with John, she scoots over a couple of feet and repeats the cleaning on the matching stone for her daughter.

SAMANTHA ANNE LAMBERT
SLEEPING WITH THE ANGELS

After both are swept free of snow and dirt, Tori takes her right leather glove off and lovingly traces her fingers over both sets of engraved writing. I hand her the bouquets, and she places the wild-flowers on John's followed by the lilies on Samantha's.

She bows her head and murmurs a prayer.

I never know what to do when we come here except offer quiet support.

Eventually, Tori stands back up and takes my hand. Side-by-side we stare out at the mountains as the sun slides behind the tallest peak.

"Thank you for coming down here with me," she says.

"Of course."

With a content smile, she finally looks at me. "It's going to be okay. Whichever way the news is about your possible son, we'll tackle it together. Just don't shut me out. This is a big deal. Don't ever be hesitant to talk to me about something, okay?"

"Okay," I say, even though she shuts me out when it comes to John and Samantha. Now is not the time to tackle that, though.

"Tell me about how all of this came to be."

And so, I do.

∼

THAT NIGHT I find Tori laying with Nathan reading him *Where are you Lydie?* It's the book he requests when he's thinking about his twin sister and dad. I pause in the door, and Tori glances up at me with moist eyes that I respond to with a gentle smile. I'm never sure if reading that book is healthy for Tori. She's always so sad afterward.

Later when the house is quiet, Tori and I lose ourselves in each other. We don't speak, but we make slow passionate love as if it's the last time we ever will.

9

The next afternoon Joanie White calls me. "It's a match. There is no doubt you are the father."

It's one thing to think it, suspect it, know it's coming, but actually hearing the words—wow. I push back from my desk and pace from my office into the living room. I stand for a moment and stare out across the fresh snow-dusted valley.

My heart thumps heavily in my chest. I breathe in. I breathe out.

"You okay?" Joanie asks.

"Yes. It's just...I have a son."

"It's a lot."

I turn away from the window. "Okay, what's next?"

"Well, as I mentioned when we met you can sign rights over to the state—"

"Absolutely not. He's mine."

"Yes, I figured you'd say that. Have you talked to your wife?"

"I did. She was understandably shocked, but we've since talked through things. We'll speak to our boys tonight. Take tomorrow to get the place ready for Francis—bed, dresser, etcetera, and Tori, that's my wife, will come with me to get Francis the following day. I'm assuming that's okay?"

"Yes. I'll text you the address of the foster family. You let me know what time, and I'll meet you there. You'll have some papers to sign, of course. Francis doesn't have much so don't worry about bringing a U-Haul or anything. I'll also want to chat with you and Tori before introducing you to Francis. There will be..."

Joanie keeps talking, running through a myriad of details. I pace the great room, listening, stopping now and then to jot a note.

Eventually, the call ends.

I text Tori. HE'S MINE.

~

THAT NIGHT my wife and I sit side-by-side on one section of the L-shaped leather couch. Nathan and Daniel sit side-by-side on the other section. To the left, the fireplace glows softly. Beyond the windows, the dark winter sky sparkles with crisp stars.

We made hamburgers and tater tots for dinner and the scent of the tots still clings in the air.

We just told them the news.

"Francis." Nathan scrunches up his face. "Isn't that a girl's name?"

"No, not necessarily," Tori says. "Some names can be both. Like Reese, Jamie, Dakota, Francis, and many more."

"Well, he can stay in my room." Nathan's legs swing back and forth. "I don't mind!"

"Good," Daniel grumbles. "Because he's not staying in mine."

"He can sleep in my top bunk! Or the bottom. I guess I should let him pick." Nathan grins. "Do you think he likes guinea pigs?"

I smile. "I'm sure Francis likes guinea pigs, and if he doesn't, you can teach him about M&M." This conversation is going much better than I thought. I glance over to Tori, but she's not smiling. She's looking at Daniel.

Who, as expected, is not taking this as exuberantly as his younger brother.

"It'll be an adjustment for all of us," I say. "The only other option is making the TV room into a bedroom. That would mean we'd bring the flat screen down into this room. But I kinda like having that TV room. Don't you all?"

"Nooo," Nathan whines. "I want him in my room."

"Eventually we'll build on," I say. "You three boys need your own space, especially as you grow older."

I start to visualize the modifications when Nathan jumps off the cushion. "Can I start making my room ready for him?"

"Sure, Buddy."

He races up the stairs and Tori quietly speaks, "Daniel, it's going to be okay. I promise."

"Are you still adopting us?" Daniel asks, looking over at the fireplace.

"Of course, I am." I can't believe he thinks otherwise.

He doesn't look at me or Tori. He simply gets up and trudges up the stairs. I look over at my wife, hoping for a reassuring word or expression, but I get nothing.

Instead, she walks over to the kitchen and pours a glass of red wine. With a mumbled, "I'll be upstairs," she leaves me alone in the great room.

~

LATER, Tori does something she hasn't done in a very long time. She takes a sleeping pill.

10

The next day I spend getting things ready for Francis, and the following day we leave to pick him up.

In my Jeep Renegade, we navigate the country roads of Rutherford County, following my GPS. "Joanie, the social worker, said he's been staying on a farm with a bunch of other kids. He's probably going to be sad to leave. They've got cows and chickens, horses and goats. Sounds like a great place."

"Mm," Tori agrees, sipping her coffee.

My fingers tap on the steering wheel. "She also said he's a little gentleman. Very polite." I laugh. "You should have seen that photo. He had a tiny bowtie. He looks just like me, Tori. It's amazing. I wonder what he likes to eat. What he likes to play. Do you think he'll be into sports? With that bowtie, he seems more scientific. Maybe I should get him a Chemistry set. There aren't any scientists on my side of the family. He must get that from his mom's side. Joanie said the trailer he grew up in had no TV, but all kinds of books and old-fashioned wooden toys. Oh, maybe he's into carpentry. Now that would be awesome. I'd love to do projects with him, ya know?"

Smiling, I glance over, but she's staring out the window at the frosty fields rolling past. Here, but not here. I wish she wouldn't have taken another sleeping pill. That's two nights in a row now.

The doctor prescribed them after John's death. At first, they worked, but soon one didn't do it and she would take two. At the time we weren't dating, but I knew what was going on. Daniel called me one night crying that his stomach hurt, and Tori wouldn't wake up. I jumped in my vehicle and drove straight over.

I saw to Daniel, made sure all was okay with Nathan, and I checked on Tori. She was breathing and her pulse beat steady, so I decided to sleep on the floor that night instead of calling 911. I checked on her every hour. When she woke in the morning and I told her what happened, she'd been mortified. Thankfully, that was the wake-up call she needed. She put the pills away and didn't take them again.

Until now.

I try to put myself in her shoes.

With Samantha's death, followed by John's, and then marrying me, it's been a roller coaster five years. Now here we are about to pick up my biological son. On the day I was supposed to sign the adoption papers, I find out about Francis.

Yes, I try to look at it from her point of view. But I'm excited, and I shouldn't feel bad about that.

She'll come around. She has to.

The GPS directs us to our last turn, speaking those final words. "You have arrived at your destination."

Here we go.

11

Kids dressed in bundled-up winter gear race across the yard, laughing and chasing each other. Being Saturday there is no school. I search each of their faces, but with their hats and scarves, I can't tell if one is Francis or not.

Off to the right, a large freshly painted green barn sits open with a tractor parked inside. Chickens scatter a sectioned-off area, pecking at the ground. Black and white cows dot the surrounding fields, most hanging out in clumps. A man dressed in overalls and a corduroy coat leads a brown horse from the barn. A handful of dirty white goats stand on the other side of a fence staring right at us.

A sprawling one-story brick and stone home follows the natural curve of the gravel driveway. My architect's eye recognizes true craftsmanship and attention to detail with the custom-built home. I park behind a white Nissan Sentra.

Joanie White steps through the front door and onto the porch. With her curly black hair pulled up in a messy bun, she wears mauve leggings and a knee-length turquoise dress. She waves. I wave back.

"That's the social worker," I tell Tori.

"She looks young."

We climb from the Jeep into the crisp morning, smelling of a wood fireplace. The sound of happy children fills the air and I smile.

"Any trouble finding the place?" Joanie asks.

"None at all." I look around, my gaze picking out the kids again. "This place is amazing."

"It is. Mr. and Mrs. Buchanan are generous people."

"How many of those kids are theirs?"

"They adopted five and they foster five at a time."

"I love that so much." With my hand gently on Tori's lower back, we ascend the stone steps up to the porch.

Joanie flashes a bright grin, just like she did when I met her at the hospital. She extends a hand to Tori. "Mrs. Grady, it is so nice to meet you."

"Likewise. Please call me Tori."

Joanie looks at me. "Are you excited?"

"Yes, of course."

She blows on her hands and sands them together. "It's cold out here. Let's go inside, have a chat, and then introduce you to Francis."

～

MINUTES later we're settled in a cozy home office, situated around a rustic wood table with Joanie and Mrs. Buchanan. Built-in floor-to-ceiling bookshelves line the walls filled with picture frames and handmade objects like a clay name plate, a carved toy, a woven potholder, a pencil sketch, a painted rock, and various other things.

A myriad of faces fills the frames, displaying a mix of ages and ethnicity, both girls and boys. A window looks out over the pasture with the cows. A desk sits in front of the window with a laptop, trays of file folders, and neatly organized office supplies. Underneath the desk is a shredder and large exercise ball that's presumably used as a desk chair.

With pixy short white hair and round flushed cheeks, Mrs. Buchanan smiles at us. "Francis is a very sweet and bright boy. He's polite and displays the mature manner of someone older. In the week he's been here, he hasn't played with the other children. He helps me in the kitchen. He sits in the living room and sews. Or, I find him in his room reading. In my conversations with him, he's rarely if ever interacted with other children. His mother raised him isolated. He doesn't know TV shows, video games, sports, popular actors, or anything. But, he knows the oddest facts."

"Like?"

"Like a fly's feet are ten million times more sensitive than a human tongue. Or that in 1980, 415 people died by ingesting oleander."

"We performed a battery of tests," Joanie says. "He's pinging above average across all sub scores. Obviously, when you go to enroll him in school, it's your call, but I suspect he'll be bored in a regular fifth-grade class, both academically and socially. Let the school see the results and make a recommendation. If it were my call, I'd recommend either gifted fifth or sixth. Definitely not the fourth grade."

Tori delicately clears her throat. "You said he doesn't play with other children. I have, we have, two sons. Twelve and five. What do you suggest?"

"Let the children figure that out. Don't stage interaction and play time. It'll happen naturally when it happens." Joanie looks between us. "Where is he sleeping?"

"With Nathan, the five-year-old. He has bunk beds and is very excited." Under the table I rest my hand on Tori's knee, giving it a comforting squeeze. "How long does it normally take for a child to transition into a new environment?"

"Every child is different," Mrs. Buchanan says. "In the week Francis has been here, he's settled in nicely. My advice is to talk to him like an adult. Don't 'dumb' things down. Brace yourself for his direct questions and manner of speaking. Introduce him to new things but also encourage his current interests. Be curious about the things that he is. Be willing to learn about what he likes."

"Did you say sewing?" I ask. "What does he sew?"

Mrs. Buchanan pushes back from the table. She crosses over to the shelves and brings down an elaborate cross-stitch of the green barn outside. She hands it to me. "This among other things."

I run a finger over the incredibly detailed thread. Sure, it's the green barn, but there's also the tractor inside and a cow in the distance, a chicken pecking the ground and a bit of snow, heck there's even a tiny farmer that must be Mr. Buchanan. "Francis did this in the week he's been here?"

"Francis did that in two days."

I show it to Tori and she nods.

"What about his things?" Tori asks. "What about the trailer and his mother's body?"

"Rachelle rented a furnished trailer. The owner has already found another renter. He boxed up what belonged to Rachelle and Francis, which amounted to mostly clothes, trinkets, books, wooden toys, sewing material, and a few baby items."

"Baby items?" I ask.

"A rattle and a onesie from when Francis was a baby, I'm sure." Joanie's ever-present smile fades a little bit. "Regarding Rachelle's body. She left specific instructions to be cremated and for her ashes to be given to Francis."

"*What*?" Tori gasps.

"Th-that's—" I shake my head. "That can't be right."

Joanie and Mrs. Buchanan exchange a look. "We were considering alternatives," Joanie says. "That is until Francis asked Mrs. Buchanan about his mom's ashes a couple of days ago. Apparently, Rachelle told him about her cremation wishes."

"Oh my God," Tori whispers.

"I know, it's a lot. You don't have to take them, but I suggest that you do. Francis may not ask you about them this week or next, but eventually, he will. It will drive an unnecessary wedge between all of you if he finds out you didn't keep his mother's ashes." Joanie pauses, giving us a moment to digest that.

I look over at Tori who is staring unblinkingly at Joanie. I don't want to take Rachelle Meade's ashes back to our home, but I'm not sure what else to do. Joanie is right. Eventually, Francis will ask about it. Based on what I've heard thus far, I suspect he'll ask sooner rather than later.

Under the table, I gently squeeze my wife's knee again. "I'll take care of storing the ashes. I'll put them in a closet or something. I'll figure it out."

Tori's eyes close. "Anything else?"

"Yes, one last thing." Joanie's lips press together, and I'm reminded of our conversation in the hospital cafeteria. There was something she wanted to tell me but didn't. "When I was first called in, I went out to the trailer. There was a dog cage in their living room. But when I asked Francis where the dog was, he simply said, 'What are you talking about? We've never had a dog.' I then asked him why they had a cage, and he changed the subject. I followed up with the owner of the trailer who replied, 'I knew something weird was going on in that place.'"

12

Mrs. Buchanan leads us through the house, talking as we go. "We've got four ovens and two stoves. It doesn't matter if we're at full capacity or not, all of our burners seem to be in use every day. Our dining room has picnic-style tables that we decorate for the season. The TV room is scheduled to eliminate fighting. Our library is stocked with the classics and most all Middle Grade and Young Adult popular series. The game room has ping pong, foosball, puzzles, and whatnot. We have two dormitory-style rooms with twin beds. One for the girls and one for the boys. Each of those rooms has matching dormitory-style bathrooms. Each child can decorate their area as they like..."

She keeps talking, walking us in and out of rooms. I try to listen, but my mind is all over the place. The ashes. My bright son. His peculiar upbringing. And the dog cage. Maybe there was a neighbor's dog that they watched. I want that to be true, but something deep in my gut says otherwise.

Mrs. Buchanan comes to a stop at an open door. Quietly, she says, "Here we are."

"Does he know I'm his father? Does he know he's leaving today?" I should've thought to ask that already.

"Francis knows he's leaving to permanently live with your family." Softly, Joanie smiles. "I left the father information to your discretion. You can tell him now or wait."

"Now." I don't hesitate. I look over to my wife who is staring in the open bedroom door. She's looking at my son. "Do you want to go with me? Or should I go in by myself?"

"I'll go in with you."

I press my palm to my heart, feeling it thump. I'm so nervous. I blow out a quiet breath. Okay, here we go. I step into a large rectangular-shaped room painted light blue. Surprisingly, it doesn't smell like the boys who live here. It smells clean like citrus.

On the left three twin beds sit spaced the same distance apart with a bulletin board hanging above their headboard. A dark brown dresser and desk take up the area in between each bed. As Mrs. Buchanan said, each child decorated their space as they liked. One comforter is white, another multi-striped, and another with footballs. One bulletin board has a calendar, another has posters of famous athletes, and another has a multitude of post-it notes. One dresser has a framed photo of a family, another a bunch of trophies, and another a pile of folded clothes. Textbooks, notebooks, calculators, papers, pencils, and pens scatter the desks.

In the back, an open door leads into a dormitory-style bathroom with multiple sinks, showers, and toilets.

The right side of the room looks the same with three beds, dressers, and desks, all done differently.

That's where I see Francis.

He sits on the center bed, propped up against the headboard, reading a book. Like in the five-by-seven photo, his blond hair lays in a neatly combed side part. He wears a buttoned-up blue shirt, a peach-colored bowtie, and khaki pants. His desk, dresser, and bulletin board are empty and ready for the next kid. Beside his twin bed, an old-fashioned tan suitcase sits closed and ready for departure.

"Francis?" I approach.

He glances up, and I lock eyes with my son for the very first time. He does look just like me. My heart squeezes.

Smiling, he closes his book. "Mr. Grady?"

His adorable, little boy voice fills me with love. "You can call me Carter, and this is my wife, Tori."

Francis comes up on his knees. He extends an arm. "I'm very pleased to meet you." He shakes both of our hands with a firm and confident grip.

I gesture to his area. "May we sit?"

"Of course." He settles cross-legged back against the headboard, I take the foot of his bed, and Tori slides into the desk chair.

Naturally, I want to talk to him as I would Nathan or Daniel, but I concentrate on having a mature tone as Joanie and Mrs. Buchanan recommended. "I'm very sad for you about your mom."

"Thank you. I'm sad too. I loved Mommy very much. But death is part of life. Someday I'll die. You'll die." Francis looks at Tori. "You will, too."

"Yes...that's true." Tori slides a glance my way.

"We're excited to meet you," I say. "We're even more excited to have you move in with us. We have two sons. Daniel is twelve and Nathan is five. You'll be sharing a room with Nathan until we're able to build onto our home. We live in East Tennessee on a ridge that overlooks the Smoky Mountains."

"I know. I, too, am excited." Francis looks at Tori again. "Carter just said, 'We have two sons.' I thought Nathan and Daniel were yours."

"How did you know that?"

"Miss White told me about the living situation. You're a lawyer and Carter is an architect. Your husband died, and you two have been married a year. She also said that Carter is in the process of adopting Nathan and Daniel."

"Yes, that's all accurate," Tori says. "We didn't realize Miss White told you so much."

Francis looks between us. "I apologize if I spoke out of turn."

"No." I shake my head. "You didn't. Their adoption hasn't gone through yet, but I still think of them as my boys."

"Do they call you 'Dad?'"

Mrs. Buchanan was not wrong about his direct way of speaking. "No, they don't. But that's okay. They'll call me 'Dad' when they're ready."

"What if they don't?"

"I'm all right with Carter," I lie. "It is my name after all."

He smiles again, keeping his focus on me. "How did you hear about me? How did you know my mom died, and that I need a new family?"

Perfect lead-in. "I knew your mom back before you were born. We met when I was in this area on business. We had a fun night together. I never knew she was pregnant with you. I only just found out last week that you exist."

"Are you saying that you and my mom had sex?"

I don't think I knew about sex at ten years old. I'm not sure if he knows what it means exactly, but that'll be a conversation for another time. "Yes, that's what I'm saying." I reach a hand over and touch his knee. "Francis, I'm your father."

His smile turns into a giant grin. "You're my daddy?"

"I am."

He crawls across the mattress and straight into my arms. I'm so shocked, I forget to hug him. Then, I do. I wrap my arms around him and hold him tight. I can't believe I'm holding my son.

"I love you, Daddy. I love you. I'm so happy you found me."

Tears spring to my eyes and I squeeze them shut. He lays his head on my shoulder, and he rocks me like I'm the child and he's the adult.

I'm not sure how long we sit here hugging, but when I open my eyes, I find Tori has left the room. In the desk chair where she was sitting lays the book Francis was reading. My gaze narrows in on the title. *As I Lay Dying*, by William Faulkner.

13

My son and I talk constantly the entire way home. I have a million questions and they surge through my mind.

Me: What do you like to eat?

Him: Meatloaf, mashed potatoes, pork chops, cheesy broccoli, oh, and almond butter!

Me: What's your favorite subject?

Him: Science and History.

Me: Do you like football, baseball, soccer...?

Him: I don't know how to do any of those, but I'm willing to learn.

Me: You didn't grow up with a TV, right?

Him: Mommy didn't want it to rot my brain.

Me: Do you like animals?

Him: I like to look at them, but I don't like to touch them.

Me: Did you help your mom with her seamstress job?

Him: Yes. I'm particularly skilled in chain stitch.

Me: I saw the barn you did for Mrs. Buchanan. You're very talented.

Him: Thank you. Do you sew?

Me: No, but I'm willing to learn. Do you like being home-schooled?

Him: Yes, but I'd like to be in a real school now if that's okay.

Me: Our town has two schools. A K through seven and an eight through twelve.

Him: What grades are Daniel and Nathan in?

Me: Daniel's in seventh. Nathan's in kindergarten.

Him: What grade will I be in?

Me: I'm not sure yet.

Him: Okay, I'm fine with whatever you think.

Me: What are your favorite books?

Him: Right now, I'm reading *As I Lay Dying*. Did you know it was banned for obscenity, abortion, reincarnation, and taking the Lord's name in vain?

Me: No, I'm not sure I did know that.

Him: Have you ever seen a dead body?

Me: Yes.

Him: You have? Where?

Me: A funeral.

Him: Oh. No, I meant like a freshly dead body.

Me: No.

Him: I have. Did you know that lips turn blue?

Me: Yes, I knew that. Regarding meatloaf—

Him: Did you know that during an abortion the doctor sucks the fetus from the woman?

Me: . . .

Him: Did you?

Me: Yes, I did know that.

Him: Did you know that in Italy it's illegal to make coffins out of anything but wood or nutshells?

Me: No, I didn't know that.

Him: Did you know that in medieval times they used to stretch people from all four directions until they split in half?

Me: . . .

Him: Did you know that back then if a woman was accused of adultery, they'd rip her breasts off?

Me: . . .

Him: Did you know they used to strap people to a wheel, spin it, and when it stopped, they'd use a hammer to crush whatever body part it stopped on.

Me: . . .

Him: Did you know they used to skin people alive?

Me: . . .

Him: Did you know they used to lock people in a coffin with rats? Then, of course, the rats would eat the person.

Me: . . .

Him: Did you know they used to hang people upside down and saw them in half?

Me: . . .

Him: Did you know there was a man who got paid to torture? What a curious and fascinating job.

Me: . . .

Did you know...

Did you know...

Did you know...

When we finally drive the ridge up to our home, Francis stops talking. I don't look over at Tori, but in my peripheral, I see her fingers clasped so tightly that the knuckles pop white. She hasn't said a word in the hours it's taken us to get home.

I feel sick.

I assume it's natural for a kid to become inquisitive about death and dying. Yet, Nathan and Daniel have never been. Then again, they didn't find their mom's dead body.

Inquisitive though isn't the right word. Fascinated? Mesmerized?

Obsessed—yes, that's the right word.

My son is obsessed with torture, death, and dying.

He begins humming, *Row, Row, Row Your Boat.*

In the rearview mirror, I glance at Francis to see him staring out the left side of the Renegade where the narrow road drops twenty feet down into a gully.

...merrily, merrily, merrily, merrily, life is but a dream.

I'm at a loss.

I've got a humming son in the back seat infatuated with mortality. His mom's ashes in my trunk. And a mute wife in the passenger seat.

All I can do is get Francis home and settled in. He's going through a phase as any kid would. It'll pass. I'm no child psychologist, but I think making a big deal about it will only escalate things. I need to introduce Francis to other topics. That'll redirect his mind.

I navigate around the last curve and our stilted wood and stone home comes into view. I glance again in the rearview. Curiosity dances through Francis' dark blue eyes, and I'm relieved to see it.

I pull under the house and put the vehicle in park. "Well, here we are."

14

Nathan barrels through the door that leads from the parking area up into the house. He rushes down the steps and straight over to Francis before any of us have had the chance to climb out.

"Hi!" He opens the door. "I'm Nathan, your brother. We're going to be sharing a room!"

I don't hide my giant smile as I glance over to Tori. Thankfully, she smiles, too. It's hard not to with Nathan.

"Hello." Francis slides out of the Jeep. He sticks his arm out, very formal like, for a shake. "I'm Francis. It's very nice to meet you, Nathan."

Nathan's smile gets even bigger as he exuberantly pumps Francis' hand. "I've got bunk beds. Do you think you'll want the top or the bottom?"

"I'm fine with either. Thank you."

Opening the back of the Renegade, I grab his old suitcase. "Let's get his things inside and then we'll worry about items like bunk beds."

"Okay!" Nathan reaches in the back, ready to help carry something—

"No!" Tori lunges forward. "I'll get that box." She snatches the ashes from his hands. "It's got something valuable in it. We can't take the chance you'll drop it." She nods to a tackle box that carries Francis' sewing things. "Take that one."

I hand the suitcase to Francis, grab the one remaining large box, and we follow Nathan up the stairs.

We find our neighbor Minnie in the kitchen laying out cookies. She lives at the bottom of the ridge and babysits when we need an extra hand. Minnie might be seventy-two, but she moves like someone in her fifties. On any given morning when I drive down to the bus stop, I find her on her front porch doing yoga. At five foot one and on the slender side, she may look petite and harmless, but she's climbed Everest, has sailed around the world, and lived for a year in the jungle.

And that's just the start. I could listen to her talk endlessly about her adventures in diving, caving, surfing, and whatever else. I hope I'm half as active as her when I get to be seventy-two.

Francis comes to a stop in the great room. He doesn't blink as he turns a slow circle, taking it all in. People who see our home for the first time tend to have this muted reaction. It really is spectacular with its open floor plan, cathedral ceiling, stone fireplace, dramatic windows, top-of-the-line appliances, granite counters, natural wood flooring, and a full wrap-around deck.

"I can't wait for you to meet M&M, that's my guinea pig. Ooh, and we have a fort in the woods. I can show it to you! Do you like gymnastics? I take classes two days a week after school. The bus stop is at the bottom of the ridge. What grade are you in? Do you like to build snowmen? How about—"

Laughing, I place the box at the bottom of the stairs. "Buddy, you've got to breathe."

"I am breathing."

"Where's Daniel?" I ask, taking the suitcase from Francis and placing it beside the box.

"In his room," Minnie says. "I yelled up that you all were home."

Francis comes back around from staring out the expansive

windows. He looks right at Tori. "This is the most beautiful home I've ever seen."

"Thank you. My husband designed it."

Francis looks at me. "You designed this?"

"I helped. John, that's Nathan and Daniel's father, he did the actual plans."

Tori clears her throat. "Yes, that's what I meant." Carrying the ashes, she heads upstairs. "I'll get Daniel."

Does it bother me she stills refers to John as her husband? Yes, but I never say anything.

Minnie walks the platter of cookies over to Francis. "Hi, I'm Minnie. I live at the bottom of the driveway."

As he's done with everyone else, he extends a hand. "I'm pleased to meet you. I'm Francis."

"My goodness, you look just like your father." Smiling, she shakes his hand.

Francis surveys me. "Yes, I suppose I do."

"That's a compliment," Minnie says. "Your dad is a good-looking man."

"Aw, shucks." I examine the cookies. "What do we have?"

"Good ole chocolate chip."

I nod for Francis to take one first, Nathan gets second, and I select one last.

While Nathan munches, he puts the tackle box down and opens it up.

"Nathan! That's not yours."

"I'm sorry." He shuts it.

"That's okay." Francis kneels next to him, reopening the box. He takes out two woven bracelets. He ties one around Nathan's little wrist. "For you."

"Oh, wow." He studies the intricate green and red thread with silver beads. "You made this?"

"I did. It means we're brothers, just like you said."

Nathan throws his arms around Francis. "Thank you!"

Footsteps tread the stairs and I glance up to see Daniel coming down followed by Tori. He stops at the landing, surveying the box, the suitcase, and then looking at Francis. He takes in his bowtie, his neatly combed hair, his buttoned-up blue shirt, and his khaki pants. "Hey."

"Hello, I'm Francis." Again, he formally extends his arm.

"Daniel." They shake.

Francis holds out the other woven bracelet. "I made this for you."

"Look!" Nathan sticks his arm out. "I got one too!"

Daniel takes it. "Thanks."

"Would you like me to put it on you?"

"No." Daniel slides it into his jeans pocket.

Over the top of Francis' head, I glare at Daniel. Would it kill him to put it on?

Tori slides an arm around his shoulders, silently telling him it's okay. Well, it's not okay. Daniel shouldn't be allowed to give Francis the cold shoulder.

Nathan grabs Francis' hand. "Come on! I want to show you our room."

15

Minnie wedges a beanie down over her long braided gray hair. "I marinated the chicken for the grill and made three-bean salad."

"Thank you, Minnie. You sure you don't want to stay for dinner?"

"Oh goodness, no." She slides her arms into a knee-length thick striped sweater. "You enjoy your first dinner as a family. We'll catch up later."

I see her to the door and hug her goodbye. After she's gone, I turn, expecting to see Tori downstairs but the area's empty. The box I carried in still sits on the landing, so I walk it upstairs. I find Daniel's door closed, our door closed, and Nathan and Francis in their room. I feel like I'm on a game show. Which door?

The thing is, I never liked game shows.

I carry the box inside the boys' room to find Nathan and Francis staring into M&M's home, or rather a mansion. That guinea lives better than most college kids. With eight square feet of area, it comes with a custom-lined bottom to protect sensitive feet and is divided into the "care" section and the "play" section. A slide and a tiny house take up the play area, but M&M only uses the slide if you physically make him slide.

Francis leans over the area and sniffs, two times, very slow.

Nathan giggles. "What are you doing?"

"Nothing, just seeing if he smells. It is a 'he,' correct?"

"That's right. Do you want to hold him?"

"No." Francis backs away.

"He won't hurt you. I play with him every night. He's never once bit me. I promise. He's actually really lazy. He doesn't move a whole lot unless you make him. He also eats just about anything you feed him." Nathan goes to unlatch the door, and Francis backs away even more.

"Nathan, he said no." I put the box down. "Some people don't like animals. You don't like snakes, right? How would you feel if Francis had a pet snake and forced you to touch it? You wouldn't like that would you?"

"No, I guess not." Nathan looks at Francis. "Sorry."

"That's okay."

I open the box. "Why don't you two start unpacking? I'll be right back."

"That one is yours." Nathan points to a dark blue dresser, and while Francis opens his suitcase, I leave them to it.

In the master bedroom, I find Tori propped on the edge of the bed staring at the box of ashes she carried up. On the nightstand, a prescription bottle sits open. Those are her anxiety meds. Like the sleeping pills, she hasn't taken one in a long time.

I close the door.

"There's something wrong with him, Carter. What ten-year-old is that fascinated with torture?" With her foot, she shoves the box with Rachelle's ashes. "We don't know anything about this woman. No one does. She raised that boy isolated from the world. What did she do to him? And what's up with the dog cage? I can't stop thinking about that." Tori looks from the ashes up at me. "I don't want him sleeping in that room with Nathan."

I look at the prescription pills. "Did you take one of those?"

"Yes." She stiffens.

Sleeping pill two nights in a row. Anxiety pill just now. I want to point it all out, but I don't. She keeps a lot of prescriptions on hand that she's accumulated over the years—sleeping, pain, muscle relaxers, anxiety, headaches, panic attacks—I get it. I do. But things have been good since we married. She hasn't taken or needed a single pill.

My mind weighs the different directions this conversation can go. I can defend my son and insist it's a phase. I can tell her how sad I am she's taking pills again. I can express my disappointment in her and Daniel's behavior—it's not them against us.

Or, I can be gentle and supportive.

I pick Rachelle's ashes up and place them next to the door. I'll figure out a spot to put them where no one knows. With a tender smile, I sit beside Tori, and I take her hand. I'm reminded of something my father said to me a long time ago.

Just tell her what she wants to hear. It's the key to a successful relationship.

I'm not sure how great that advice is, but I choose to take it. "I am on your side, Tori. Never doubt that. It's not me and Francis against you and the boys. This has thrown all of us. There will be an adjustment. It will take patience." I press a kiss to the back of her hand. "I'm so sorry this has happened. Know that I agree with you. The way Francis was raised has formed him into an odd little boy. The first thing on my list is to make an appointment for him with a psychologist. We need to know exactly what we're dealing with. I don't know about you, but I feel out of my element with him. I also plan on hiring a private investigator to look into Rachelle Meade."

She breathes out, and her shoulders drop with relief. "I'm so glad you see it, too."

"As far as sleeping with Nathan, it would crush him if we took Francis from their room. Nathan is so dang excited about all of this."

She thinks about that for a second. "Yeah, you're right."

I kiss her hand again. "All three do need their own room, though. I'll begin drafting those plans tomorrow to build on."

She lays her head on my shoulder and we stay that way for a quiet moment. Something in the air shifts as her body eases into relaxation. I suspect the pill kicked in.

Another moment goes by and she reaches under the bed, sliding out a wrapped package. "I bought it for Francis. It's a scrapbook where he can build new memories."

"I love that so much." I hug her.

She snaps the cap back on the pill box. "Why don't you get dinner going and I'll help Francis unpack? Do you mind if I go ahead and give him the gift?"

"Sounds great." I smile.

Tori kisses my cheek and carrying the wrapped scrapbook, she leaves the room. She doesn't even pause as she passes Rachelle's ashes.

The door closes, and my smile slides away.

I hate that I just lied to my wife.

16

Other than Daniel's continued sulking, dinner goes better than expected.

"Tomorrow is Sunday," Tori says. "We typically go to church. How about instead I make everyone breakfast. What do you like Francis?"

"Oh, I'm not picky. I eat everything."

"That's good to hear. Daniel's the same way." I cut Nathan a playful look. "You could learn a thing or two on that topic."

He grins.

"I thought you'd have more clothes." Tori cuts into the marinated chicken. "How about I take you shopping tomorrow afternoon? You'll need some things for school."

Francis wipes his mouth. "I'm fine with hand-me-downs if Daniel has old clothes."

"I don't have any old clothes," Daniel grumbles.

"No, no, no. We'll get you some new things." Tori smiles. "I saw that you have an old Polaroid camera. I didn't realize they still made film for those. What types of items do you like to take pictures of?"

"Just things." Francis drinks his sweet tea. "Humans. Animals. Places. Whatever draws my interest, I suppose."

"Well, I'd love to see your photos if you want to share." Tori eats the chicken she cut. Francis smiles. She smiles.

"Can I show Francis the fort tomorrow?" Nathan asks.

"Of course, you can." I look at Daniel. "Maybe your brother will want to go to."

"That's a fabulous idea!" Tori exuberantly says, and I wonder how many pills she took. "Breakfast, then you boys explore, then we'll all go to town for shopping. Is there anything you need for the room?" she asks Francis.

"No, ma'am. I have everything I need." He looks right at Daniel. "You're coming with us to the fort?"

"I guess." He shrugs.

The conversation continues with Tori doing the majority of the talking, Francis responding, and Nathan jumping in here and there. Daniel remains quiet, eating and staring at his plate.

After dinner, Francis offers to clean the kitchen.

"Why don't you boys enjoy some TV time?" Tori says. "We've got the kitchen."

They disappear upstairs, and Tori looks right at me. "I don't know what I was worried about. Mrs. Buchanan was right. He's a sweet boy."

Yes, she took more than one pill.

17

The sound of gunfire leads me into the TV room where I find all three boys sitting on the carpet in front of the wide flat TV.

Aside from the video game currently on the screen, darkness engulfs the room. Two milk chocolate-colored recliners and two matching bean bags sit empty.

They don't notice as I slide into a recliner. This isn't a game Nathan is allowed to play, but I let it pass this one time.

Daniel shoots a zombie from a brick wall. "Yes, take that!" He fires again. This time a zombie splatters into a blobby mess.

Nathan cringes.

Francis watches with unblinking dead-set eyes.

Another zombie liquefies. Daniel misses the next one, and it eats him.

"Dang!" He glances over to Francis who still hasn't blinked. "What, you've never played this before?"

"No, we didn't have a TV."

"What? How is that possible? That's weird." He hands Francis the controller. "You'll move with these buttons. Fire with this one. Kill as many zombies as you can. That's all there is to it."

"That's a big gun he's holding."

"Yep." Daniel launches a new game. "Okay, see where it says, 'GET OFF THE ROOF.' That's your instructions. Those will pop up as you go. Got it?"

Francis nods. He moves across the roof and kicks the door open. A zombie pops up.

"Kill it!" Daniel yells.

He fires. The zombie falls. Francis moves toward another door. It opens, and a family of flesh-eaters pours out. He fires a sweeping line of bullets, and they fly to the side. One isn't quite dead, and he shoots it right between the eyes. Blood splatters the screen, dripping down in a gooey mess. He races right past the pile of dead bodies, takes a flight of steps down, kicks open the next door, and zombies attack. Bang. Bang. Bang. He expertly takes them out.

The game continues, I stop watching it and look instead at my son's face. Gone is the wide-eyed curiosity to be replaced by a focus so deeply intense I doubt anything would make him lose his concentration.

Bang. Bang. Bang.

More zombies are dead.

"Holy shit, you're good," Daniel says.

I clear my throat. "Language."

All three boys look away from the TV, now realizing I'm in the room too.

Francis slowly puts the controller down. Curiosity once again replaces the deep intensity. He stands. "I'm ready for bed. Daddy, will you tuck me in?"

PART II

Francis

18

M y new parents make breakfast—waffles, bacon, and sliced pineapple. Daniel likes me now that I can kill zombies, and he talks non-stop through our morning meal about game strategy. Daddy and New Mommy seem both amused and pleased. I read that shared experience brings people together.

Killing zombies is our shared experience.

"Can we show him the fort now?" Nathan asks.

"Sure, Buddy. Be back in an hour. We're all going to town." Daddy waves a hand over the messy table. "Just leave it."

I smile at New Mommy. "Thank you for breakfast. It was delicious."

"You're welcome. Bundle up. It's cold out."

At the door, we pause to put coats, gloves, and hats on. I'm not an outdoor person, but my new brothers seem to be, so I go with it. I'd rather stay inside and help clean up.

Nathan and Daniel race out the door, across the porch, and down onto the frozen ground. They sprint away from the house and along the ridge through the icy trees.

I follow.

It's cold out this morning, and I open my mouth wide, huffing hard just to see the condensation gather.

Breathing heavy, my new brothers come to a stop at a large sturdy tree. Daniel looks up through the branches. "See! Isn't it awesome? Carter helped us build it."

A planked ladder has been nailed into the trunk, weaving its way up twenty feet or so to a triangular wooden fort built around the tree. Stilts hold it up, nailed at an angle from the bark to the corners of the fort. A rope dangles off the side where you can slide down like a fireman's pole. Windows with thick glass look out all three sides. I note a harness and pulley system.

"That's for Nathan," Daniel says, seeing where I'm looking. "He's not allowed up without it."

"What about me?" I ask.

Daniel scoffs. "What, are you scared of heights?"

"Are you?"

"Whatever." He looks at Nathan. "Stay here for a second. I want to show Francis something."

"What? Why?" Nathan whines. "It's not *your* fort. It's *our* fort."

Daniel ignores him, climbing the rungs up. He disappears through a trap door into the fort.

I take a second to unlatch the harness from the bottom rung. I give the karabiner and rope pulley system a study. "How does this work?"

"I don't know." Nathan shrugs. "Ask Carter. It breaks my fall if I slip."

"Really? How do you know?"

"Carter said."

"You've never tried."

"No. I've never slipped."

"You coming or what?" Daniel looks down at me through the trap door.

I hand the harness to Nathan, and I climb at a slower pace, looking around as I go. I see why they put the fort here. It's visible from the house, which is exactly what my new parents are doing. They're standing on the porch watching us.

I thought they were cleaning.

One last rung and I disappear into the triangular little home, complete with a roof tall enough that we can stand.

A hammock hangs across one corner. A pirate wheel takes up the other corner. The third contains shelves with junk. Two lawn chairs lay folded and propped against the far wall.

I look out the first window to once again see my new home. My new parents are still standing there, but now they're hugging and not looking this way. The second window shows the driveway up along the ridge. The third looks out over the valley.

It's as I'm looking out that window that the sun glints off something in the ground. I point. "What's that?"

Daniel glances at it before taking a tin box off the shelves. "Graves." He slides a key from his back jeans pocket and unlocks the tin.

"What kind of graves?"

"My dad and little sister are buried there."

"Little sister?"

"Nathan's twin." He opens the box. "This is what I wanted to show you." Inside sits a pack of cigarettes, a lighter, and naked pictures of women.

"How did your dad die?"

"Kayaking accident."

"Did you see the body?"

He doesn't answer.

"How did your sister die?"

Daniel stops fiddling with the box and stares at me. "What the hell kind of questions are those?"

"I'm sorry. My mommy died recently. I saw her dead body."

"Oh...that's...that's bad."

"Her lips were blue. Do you think all dead people have blue lips?"

Daniel keeps staring at me.

I wait for him to answer, but he doesn't. I look at the tin box. "What do you want to show me?"

"Um, just this. We can come here and smoke. And..." He holds up a picture of a naked woman that's been cut from a magazine.

"Okay."

"Okay?"

Nathan pops his head up through the trap door and Daniel hurriedly puts everything back.

"I told you to stay down there!" Daniel yells.

Nathan comes to a stop on the top rung. "You're not the boss of me."

I look again at the harness, now fastened to Nathan, and the pulley system. From up here, the rope can be untied, and the pulley wouldn't work anymore. Looks like there's some sort of weight, too. Interesting. I stare past him down to the ground. That's a long way.

What would happen if one of us fell? Would we break something, or would we die?

Probably break something. It'd have to be further for death. Unless it's something tiny like M&M.

Then again, Nathan's pretty tiny.

Either way, he's never slipped. He doesn't know for sure if the pulley works. We should probably find that out.

He's still balanced on the top rung. Daniel's back is to us as he fiddles with the tin box, trying to lock it back.

Nathan lets go of the ladder to climb the rest of the way up, and I reach down and push him.

His scream echoes across the ridge.

19

"I don't understand." Daddy glares at Daniel.

Nathan snuggles into New Mommy. She hugs him tight, rubbing his back, shushing him. I wish she'd hug me. I miss my mommy's hug.

"I don't know. I wasn't looking." Daniel glances at me.

"It was my fault," I say. "I reached down to help Nathan, but he lost hold and fell. The harness caught him, though. It works. We should all be happy to know that, right?"

New Mommy keeps hugging Nathan. She looks at Daddy with concern. Why is she concerned? Nathan's fine. The harness caught him. He's not broken.

Or dead.

Daddy kneels in front of him. "Buddy, are you sure you're okay?"

He sniffs and nods, finally looking at me. But his eyes are different. They're not happy and excited, they're suspicious and scared.

I copy Daddy as I kneel in front of my new little brother. "I'm sorry I lost hold of you. It was an accident. I won't ever let anything happen to you. Big brothers are supposed to protect little brothers, right?"

He doesn't answer.

"Well, I'm your big brother. So is Daniel. It's our job to protect you."

"Daniel's older than you," Nathan mumbles.

Daddy says, "Which means Daniel has an even bigger job. He has to protect both of you."

"Who do I protect?" Nathan asks.

"M&M," Daddy says.

Finally, Nathan stops hugging New Mommy. I look into his eyes, pleased to see the fear gone, yet disappointed the happiness still isn't back.

I hold open my arms. "Will you forgive me?"

"Okay." Quickly he hugs me, and just as quickly he steps away.

That's okay. By the end of the day, he'll believe that I lost hold.

∾

THE REST of Sunday I focus on Nathan. Everything he did yesterday when I first arrived, I do back.

I hold his hand as we go to Target and buy new clothes.

I talk to him as we go to an indoor farmer's market.

I laugh with him as we go to a park and play.

I playfully poke him as we go to a restaurant and eat.

I'm excited. I'm happy. My whole world is Nathan.

New Mommy doesn't think I see her, but she cautiously watches me and Nathan the entire day.

By the time we get home, my new little brother is back to normal. Just like I knew he would be.

And now here I lay on the top bunk with Nathan on the bottom. We're supposed to be asleep.

He giggles. "Today was fun."

"It was."

"I wish every day could be like today."

Daddy comes through the open door, dressed in pajamas. "You two are supposed to be asleep."

We giggle.

Smiling, New Mommy comes in too. She wears a thick white robe tied tightly. Daddy kisses me on the forehead while New Mommy kisses Nathan. Then they switch positions.

New Mommy doesn't kiss me, but she trails her fingers through my hair as she looks at me. Her touch feels so good I almost close my eyes, but I don't. I want to look at her.

Daddy and New Mommy are very different. He's been eager and welcoming since the moment I met him. New Mommy seems to be all over the place. Stand-offish, overly happy, willing to try, concerned, cautious, and now I get the sense she's wobbling between all of them.

And after all my hard work today with Nathan. I don't get it. What do I have to do?

A shared experience, that's what we need.

I look at the front of her tied robe where it overlaps to cover her chest. She shifts away, but I open my arms as I lean forward from the top bunk.

Hesitantly, she hugs me.

But I hold tight. "I love you, Mommy."

20

The next morning Daddy parks the Jeep in the school lot. The four of us climb out.

Nathan hugs me. "Have a good first day, Big Brother."

Smiling, I hug him back. I open my arms for Daniel and he takes a step away. "Dude, I'm not hugging you."

With that, he walks off to join some boys who are waiting for him. He says something to them, and they all laugh.

Nathan waves goodbye and runs in the opposite direction.

Daddy beeps the Jeep to lock it. He points to the right where Nathan went. "Kindergarten through third are in those buildings." He points to the left where Daniel went. "Fourth through seventh are in those buildings. The two sides are connected here in the center with shared spaces like the gym and cafeteria. You'll be on Daniel's side."

"Will I see Nathan throughout the day?"

"Maybe. Depends on what's going on around school."

I survey the octagon-shaped brick buildings. I can't believe I'm about to go to a real school.

Kids hurry past me, some looking at me and others not. A bell rings.

Daddy leads the way across the parking lot and into a door.

Rolling my brand-new book bag behind me, I ask, "How come Mommy didn't come?"

"She had to go to work. I work from home, so my schedule's more flexible." He puts a hand on my shoulder. "By the way, Tori has diamond earrings that she can't find. Keep a look out, please. They belonged to her grandmother. It's not that they're expensive. They're more sentimental."

"She was wearing diamond earrings on Saturday when you two came to get me from Mrs. Buchanan."

Daddy gives me an odd look. "You noticed that?"

"Of course. They were bright and pretty."

He opens a glass door with the words ADMINISTRATION stenciled across it. "Well, anyway, keep a look out."

"Okay." I stand beside Daddy as he checks us in. We only have to wait a few minutes, and then we're led into an office labeled COUNSELOR.

An old man wearing a burgundy sweater vest and silver striped tie greets us. "I'm Dr. Dixon, it is very nice to meet you, Francis."

I shake his hand, noting the dryness of his skin. "It's very nice to meet you too." I sniff the air. "I like your cologne."

"Thank you." He motions toward a round table with leather chairs. "Please take your jackets off and be comfortable."

On the table sits one thin file folder. I stare at it as I unbutton my navy wool coat and drape it over the back of a chair.

Dr. Dixon looks straight at my bowtie, and his lips twitch when he notes I wear a sweater vest too. "Aren't you the dapper dresser," he says.

I'm not sure what dapper means, but he's wearing a sweater vest, too, so I say, "As are you."

He chuckles, folding his hands on top of the file. I note his manicured fingernails. "I am the school counselor and also the district psychologist. I'll be overseeing your transition to your new family and school. I've—"

"District Psychologist. That's what Miss White said she wanted to be. She'll be a doctor soon. She told me that, too. Does that mean she'll get your job?"

Dr. Dixon looks at Daddy and then back to me. "Well, I have my job. I'm sure when she gets her doctorate, there will be other district psychologist jobs she can apply for throughout the state."

"I like Miss White," I say. "She's pretty."

He smiles. "I'm glad to hear you like Miss White. Speaking of Joanie, we had a conversation, and I also reviewed the file she sent over. Taking into account academic and social factors, we feel you'll be best suited in the fifth-grade gifted class."

"I'm not sure what that means, but it sounds good to me."

"Are you excited to come to school?"

"Yes, sir."

"I'm glad. We've got good kids here. We have a no-tolerance policy for bullying. Do you know what that means?"

"Kids are not allowed to be mean to each other."

"Correct." He smiles at me.

I fold my hands on top of the table, mirroring his. "I'm a good boy. You won't ever have to worry about me."

21

"Class, this is Francis, and he's just moved here from Murfreesboro." My teacher, Mrs. Espy, smiles down at me. She's old and chubby with fake blonde hair and fat cheeks. "I don't want to put you on the spot, but you're welcome to say something if you'd like."

I look across the faces of the boys and girls in my fifth-grade class. Some smile. Others look on bored. I put on my best manners as I say, "Hello, I'm very happy to be here. I've never been to a real school. I look forward to being friends with you. I'm also very smart. If you need help with work, just let me know." I look at Mrs. Espy. "I guess that's it."

She points to a desk positioned in the first row, third back. I wheel my book bag across the room, smiling as I go. Everyone watches but no one says a word. I drape my wool coat over the seat, and I slide into my very own desk.

Dr. Dixon said I'd have the same teacher all day long. Next year, in the sixth, I'll have different teachers for different subjects. I think I might like that even better.

While Mrs. Espy begins passing out paperback novels, I unzip my book bag and take out my brand-new pencil case and multi-subject notebook that we bought yesterday at Target. Cubby holes line the back wall of the room with names attached, each one stuffed with books, lunchboxes, and extra school supplies. I hope I get one of those cubby holes. It'll be easier than keeping my things in this wheeled bag. For now, though, I zip the bag back together and lay it down beside my desk.

I position the pencil case at a ninety-degree angle in the top left corner of my desk top. The notebook I square off in the center. Linking my fingers, I straighten my back, and I look up. All around me my new friends silently stare.

Maybe I was supposed to introduce myself. I don't want them to think I'm rude. I hold my hand out to the boy beside me. "Hi, I'm Francis. It's very nice to meet you."

He doesn't do anything. He just stares at my hand.

That's not very polite. Someone needs to teach him manners.

Mrs. Espy rounds the desks in the back, still handing out paperback books. "We left off on chapter three…"

I repeat, holding my hand out to the girl who sits diagonal to me. She quickly looks away, pretending not to notice my gentlemanly gesture. I glance around the kids in my area of the classroom, and they all look away too.

Old Mommy said she didn't want me going to a real school because kids wouldn't understand me and would be mean.

"Maia, remind the class what happened at the end of chapter two."

The girl in front of me begins speaking and her voice draws my focus. She has long, red hair and it hangs down between our two desks. Old Mommy had hair just like that.

I miss Old Mommy.

Reaching out, I comb my fingers through the thick strands just like I used to do with Old Mommy. I wish I had her brush.

"Oh my God!" Maia leaps from her chair. "He just touched me!" She jabs her finger at me. "That freak just ran his fingers through my hair!"

~

Freak.

What's up with the bowtie?

I'm also very smart.

Pervert.

Hi, I'm Francis.

The rest of my first day of real school didn't go well. No one spoke to me unless they were mimicking me or calling me names.

During lunch, someone hit me with a spitball. I was moved to a desk in the back corner of the room. When all the kids went outside to play, I had to see Dr. Dixon.

"Francis, you're not allowed to touch other kids," he says. "Do you understand?"

"You said the kids here were good."

"They are good kids."

I look away from Dr. Dixon's face. "No, they're not," I murmur.

He either doesn't hear me or he ignores me. "Do you understand about not touching?" he asks again.

But I like touching, I want to say. Instead, I nod.

Old Mommy was right. I don't like real school.

22

That night I sit on my bedroom floor watching M&M watch me. Nathan's in the bath and Daniel's in his room doing homework. Daddy and New Mommy are downstairs cleaning up from dinner.

They want to talk to me in a few minutes about what happened at school.

In the far corner of M&M's area sits an empty bowl. This morning that bowl had chunks of carrots and broccoli in it. Yesterday it had peas and lettuce. Nathan said he also eats hay and artichokes and whatever else.

I glance over to my dresser where I stashed New Mommy's diamond earrings. I wonder if M&M would eat those, too. I'll have to try that soon.

On the floor beside me lays the open workbook and pencil where I just finished my homework. I pick the sharpened pencil up and I rotate it eraser out. "You never move." I nudge M&M in the rear. "Move."

He does nothing. Just keeps staring at me.

Again, I nudge him with the eraser, this time harder. "Move."

Still, he doesn't.

I rotate the pencil, sharpened-end out, and I poke him in the butt. He moves, sliding forward not even an inch. I go again, this time harder, watching the pencil tip burrow into his fur.

He shrieks so loudly that I jump back.

My heart hops around in my chest as I watch M&M move quickly to tuck into the tiny house next to the slide.

"Francis?" Daddy calls from downstairs. "Can you come down?"

"Coming!" I scramble to retrieve the pencil and on a last thought, I wave the pointed edge back and forth in front of the opening to the tiny house just to see what he does.

M&M scoots further back, and I smile.

Looks like I figured out how to make him move.

~

ON THE LANDING of the stairs, I look out the wall of windows to see New Mommy carrying a flashlight and walking away from the house down the valley toward the graves.

I want to see the graves.

"Francis, come on over here."

With a smile, I join Daddy on the soft leather couch. "Isn't Mommy going to talk to me too?"

"No, just me. She wanted some alone time."

"Oh, okay." Crossing my right leg over my left, I fold my hands on top of my knees. "You'd like to talk about today at school, correct?"

"Yes. I know what happened from your teacher and Dr. Dixon. But I'd like to hear about it from you."

"I introduced myself to a few of them, but they ignored me. I touched Maia's hair and that's when I got in trouble."

"Tell me why you touched her hair."

"Because it reminded me of Mommy's red hair."

"I see." He shifts forward, bracing his elbows on his knees. He taps his fingers together, looking into the fireplace.

"Can you teach me here like Mommy used to teach me? I decided I don't like real school."

"I can't. I'm sorry." He looks at me. "The way you've been raised thus far has made you into a bright and curious, unique boy. You're not sure how to act around other kids, and the adults understand that. Today wasn't a very good day for you, but I'd like to see you go back and try again. It's important that you spend time with children, and not just Daniel and Nathan. Others, too. Try watching the kids in your class. See how they act around each other. At night we can talk about it and discuss what's appropriate and what's not."

"Can I take notes?"

"Sure, if you want."

I like the thought of watching and keeping notes. Especially if they don't know I'm doing it. "Okay, I can do that."

"Also, Dr. Dixon wants to begin seeing you two times a week."

"About what?"

"Whatever you want to talk about. Me, your new family, the move, your old life..."

⁓

An hour later New Mommy comes in to read Nathan a bedtime story. She crawls into the bottom bunk and Nathan snuggles into her arms.

I lay quietly in the top bunk sucking my thumb and listening to her soft voice as she reads the pages.

Old Mommy read to me every night while I had my nightly milk. Will New Mommy read to me when she's done with Nathan? I hope so.

Her voice gradually dies as Nathan drifts off into dreams. I fight my own sleep, waiting for my turn. But when New Mommy finishes, she doesn't come to me. Instead, she tiptoes across the room, turns off the red desk lamp, and leaves.

Minutes tick by and I continue sucking my thumb, waiting for her to return. But she doesn't.

I listen to Nathan's deep breaths. I smell the fabric softener of my sheets. I stare at the crack in the bedroom door.

Still, she doesn't return.

Lonely tears fill my eyes. I need New Mommy.

With a quiet sniff, I crawl from the top bunk careful not to wake Little Brother. I continue sucking my thumb as I follow the hallway light past Daniel's room and our shared bathroom. I come to a stop at my new parents' bedroom door.

More tears come.

Gently, I turn the knob and the door silently inches inward. A light on the inside of the gun cabinet illuminates the room. On the king-size bed, New Mommy lays naked with her legs spread and Daddy's head between them. She moans, arching up.

I stand in the shadows, sucking my thumb, quietly crying and watching.

23

———————

The next morning, I go downstairs to find New Mommy putting a long red coat on. Daddy loops a soft white scarf around her neck, tugging her in for a kiss.

"Last night was fabulous," he whispers.

"Agreed." She smiles.

She looks so pretty this morning with lips that match her coat and dark bangs that brush her black-framed glasses.

"Mommy?"

Startled, she pulls away from Daddy. "Francis, I didn't see you there."

"You look so very pretty," I say.

"Thank you."

I cross the great room over to the mud area and I nudge between them. I hug her waist tight, burying my face into her breasts. My eyes warm with tears, and I squeeze her tight. She smells like the most delicious perfume of all perfumes.

"You smell nice," I sigh.

"Um..." She pats my back and it feels so good.

"Tonight, will you read to me like you did Nathan?" I melt into her.

She pats my back again. "Okay."

"Thank you." I kiss her coat where it crosses over her breasts. "Thank you, Mommy."

~

AT SCHOOL, I do exactly what Daddy suggested. I watch the other kids and I take detailed notes of what I see in a brand new black and silver striped spiral notebook.

Like when Maia, the red-haired girl, passes notes with the boy who sits beside her.

Or when Mrs. Espy leans over and her big pink panties show through her white pants.

Like when pretty girls at lunch share lip gloss.

Or when I go to the bathroom and find Daniel and another boy smoking a cigarette.

"You're not supposed to be doing that," I say.

The other boy flushes it. "Get out of here, you idiot."

"You tell and you're dead." Daniel levels me with a challenging glare.

"You're my brother. You're supposed to like me."

The other boy looks me up and down. "This is him?" He snorts a laugh. "You don't look like you can kill zombies." He nudges Daniel. "You should totally get your BB gun. See what your brother here can do with a real target."

"He's not my bro—"

The door opens and in walks Dr. Dixon. He sniffs the air. "What's going on in here?"

Daniel and the other boy exchange a look. "Nothing," Daniel says. "We were just leaving."

They walk past Dr. Dixon, leaving me alone. He looks right at the striped spiral notebook I'm carrying. "What's that?"

I tell him about it.

"Your father is a smart man to suggest that. You can also write about your old life before you came to live here."

I like that idea. But, "I don't have to show anyone the notebook, right? It's private?"

"It's your property. Many people write their private thoughts in a journal. You don't have to share it unless you want to." He smiles. "I'd like to start meeting with you regularly."

"Yes, Daddy told me."

"Can we chat later today?"

"Sure."

Dr. Dixon leaves, and I open my notebook. I flip to the back and start a new section about Old Mommy. I label it KITTY because some nights that's what I called her.

24

I like riding the school bus. I sit in front next to Nathan just two seats back from the driver. Her name is Sally-Anne. She's short and skinny, and everyone is afraid of her. She can shoot any kid a glare in the big rearview mirror and they'll immediately shut up.

Sally-Anne is my new favorite person. She's mean to mean kids.

"Bye," I say as I take the steps down off her bus. "Until tomorrow, Ms. Sally-Anne."

She smiles and winks. That means I'm a good kid.

Daddy's waiting in his Jeep along with all the other parents here to pick up their kids. Our bus stop services the surrounding homes and farms. Nearly twenty kids get off at this bus stop, leaving Sally-Anne with only two stops left before she goes home.

Daniel climbs in the front passenger side leaving the back for me and Nathan. As Little Brother begins rapidly telling Daddy about his day, we drive the ridge up to our home. We pass Minnie's house and she waves us down as she runs across her frozen yard to the Jeep.

Daddy rolls his window down.

"Have you all seen Boots?" she asks.

"No," Daddy says. "We'll keep a lookout though."

"Thanks." She sweeps a concerned smile over us before turning away.

Daddy rolls his window up and keeps driving.

"Maybe we'll get lucky and it's dead," Daniel mumbles.

"Daniel." Daddy shakes his head. "Not nice."

"Who is Boots?" I ask.

"Minnie's cat. He's black with white feet, and he's a nightmare. No one likes him. If you see him, don't try to pet him. He bites. He scratches. He growls. Minnie is the only person who he's nice to."

"Like Jekyll and Hyde," I say.

Daddy looks at me in the rearview mirror. "You know Jekyll and Hyde?"

"Yes, Mommy and I read the story together."

"What's Jekyll and Hyde?" Nathan asks.

"It's about a person with two personalities," Daddy says as he pulls under our house. "A good versus an evil type of thing."

"Hyde has this sneering coolness, like the devil himself." I unbuckle my seatbelt. "He can make someone uncomfortable just by looking at them. He's malevolent. He's spiteful. He's corrupt and complicated. He's *amazing*."

Daddy looks at me in the rearview mirror.

"I don't know what all that means," Nathan says.

"I don't either." Daniel opens his door. "Plus, I'm bored. Let's go."

With a shrug, I open my door and step out.

Daddy clears his throat. "I made banana bread if anyone's hungry."

"Can I go to the fort?" Daniel asks.

"Ooh, me too!" Nathan says.

"No," Daniel groans.

Daddy shuts his door. "Why don't you three find something to do together?"

"We could shoot that BB gun your friend mentioned." I'd rather eat banana bread, but I want Daniel to like me. So far, my expertise with zombies is the only reason why he does. Maybe I'll be just as good with a BB gun.

∿

WE'VE BEEN OUTSIDE forty-five minutes shooting at metal targets set up around the front yard. Daddy spent fifteen minutes giving me a safety lecture, another fifteen coaching me on sighting and firing, and another fifteen on the actual shooting.

"I'm bored," Nathan complains.

I am too, I want to say but Daniel seems enthralled with my talent. What's the big deal, you sight and shoot?

"Dude, you hit it again!" Daniel throws his hands up. "How do you do it?"

"I don't know." I shift to the left, narrow in on a bright red bulls-eye, and pull the trigger. It pings off the center, triggering it to swing up.

Daniel takes the BB rifle, shoots, and misses.

Nathan whines. "Carter, can I have banana bread now?"

Daddy looks at me. "You seem to have the hang of it. All good if I take the kid inside?"

"Can I go in too?"

"No!" Daniel puts the gun back in my hand. "Just a couple more. Please?" He races away to put one of the metal targets at a greater distance.

"Five more minutes." Daddy winks, just like Ms. Sally-Anne did. "Then you're relieved of duty."

While he and Nathan walk up the exterior steps to the side door, Daniel runs around the yard resetting the targets. Maybe if they were moving, I'd have more fun.

More challenge.

A low and cold wind kicks up, snaking along my neck. With a shiver, I hunch my shoulders and lift the rifle to sight. Through the scope, I follow Daniel around the yard. My trigger finger twitches as I imagine pinging him in the leg. The back. The arm. The head.

I wonder if a BB pellet even hurts.

He kneels, righting a target, and I move the scope beyond him to the frozen and spindly trees. With my right eye closed, I zero in on a thin branch moving in the breeze. My finger triggers and a second later the skinny branch breaks free.

That's a pretty strong BB.

Something moves in my peripheral and I swing the scope to the right. My gaze collides with two tiny green eyes surrounded by black fur. I look at his white feet. *Well, hello, Boots.* Even though fifty yards separate us, he hisses at me.

Eeny, meeny, miny, moe. Left eye. Right eye. Left eye. Right eye.

Left it is.

I aim, and I shoot.

With a loud screaming howl, Boots leaps from the branch and races through the trees away from our home. I watch him through the scope the whole way. He'll have to be re-named to One-Eyed-Boots now.

I smile.

Here kitty, kitty, kitty.

But One-Eyed-Boots is long gone. Perhaps he'll be a little nicer now.

When I lower the gun, I see Daniel staring at me.

"Maybe we'll get lucky and it's dead," I repeat his words from earlier.

He doesn't say anything back.

I lift the gun again, and I look at Daniel through the scope.

He swallows. "Put that down."

Shifting to the left, I ping a metal target behind him. Daniel jumps.

Calmly, I walk the gun over to him. "I didn't mean to hit Boots. You know that right? It was an accident."

Slowly, he nods.

"Besides, brothers keep secrets. I'll keep your smoking secret. You keep this one." I hand him the gun. "Cool?"

"C-cool."

25

That night after dinner, Daddy builds a fire. He settles into the corner of the couch to read. Daniel and Nathan disappear upstairs into the TV room. New Mommy's in the kitchen making brownies. I retrieve my sewing box from my bedroom closet and after joining Daddy in front of the fireplace, I begin a new cross-stitch project.

Silently I work, listening to the fire crackle and smelling the brownies baking in the kitchen.

Eventually, New Mommy comes over to join us near the fire. On the coffee table, she places the scrapbook that she bought me. "I thought we might work on this tonight."

"Okay."

I lay my new project aside. She glances at it. "What are you making?"

"A present for Minnie. It's Boots."

"How do you know what Boots looks like?" she asks.

Daddy says, "We ran into Minnie earlier. Boots is missing."

"He'll come back. He always does," she grumbles, and they share a laugh.

From under the coffee table, New Mommy retrieves a bucket of craft supplies complete with markers, stickers, glue, glitter, and various other things. She sets it next to the scrapbook. "It's your book. You should decorate it how you'd like."

"Do you have any suggestions?"

"Why don't you make your first couple of pages about your life before you came to live with us?"

I like that idea. Grabbing a green colored pencil, I slide onto my knees in front of the coffee table. In the upper left corner of the first scrapbook page, I draw the green floral dress that Old Mommy used to wear. It was her favorite. I take extra care to darken the hem and shade the flowers.

Next, I select a black pencil and outline the trailer where we lived. I start to draw Old Mommy and I stop.

I start again, and I stop.

Again, and stop.

With an unhappy grunt, I scribble through the trailer and I rip the page from the scrapbook. I ball it up and throw it into the fire. The flames lick and ignite.

Closing my eyes, I breathe in and back out. My meager talent can't do Old Mommy justice. I need the actual thing.

I lift the top tray from my sewing box and set it aside. The second tray doesn't come out, but I pull it up and lock its hinge. Hidden underneath, I find what I'm looking for—a stack of Polaroids rubber-banded together.

With the rubber band still on, I hold them close to my chest and I finger through them until I find the one I want—a Polaroid of Old Mommy sitting in a rocking chair hand stitching a blanket. The rest I put back into the bottom of the sewing box and close it up.

I select a glue stick from the bucket of supplies and I paste it centered on the first new page. Perfect. With a smile, I look up to see Daddy and New Mommy staring at me.

"Where are the ashes?" I ask.

Daddy nods to the sewing box. "Can I see the pictures you put back in there?"

"No." I keep my smile in place. "Where are the ashes?"

New Mommy clears her throat.

"Why do you want them?" Daddy asks.

"Why does it matter?" My smile falters. "Are you going to tell me where they are or not?"

My new parents exchange a look. Daddy puts his book aside and gets up. "I'll get them for you." He crosses the great room and goes out the door that leads down under the house where they park their cars.

While I wait, I find gold glitter in the bucket. "Can I have an old bowl and plastic spoon?"

New Mommy walks into the kitchen and comes back with a small square Tupperware singed on the corner from being in the microwave too long. She hands me that and a plastic spoon.

"Thank you." Into the Tupperware, I squeeze a generous amount of glue. On top, I sprinkle gold glitter.

Daddy returns carrying a cardboard box. He places it on the coffee table.

I glance at it. "Open it please."

He does, using a utility knife to cut through the tape. He wedges the flaps back to reveal a clear bag inside with gray ashes.

"I take it Mommy was outside in the cold?"

"Yes."

"That makes me sad." I motion Daddy aside, and I peel open the plastic bag.

Nathan comes downstairs. "Mommy, can I—"

"Not now," she's quick to say.

"But—"

"Not. Now."

With a sigh, he stomps back upstairs.

I scoop the plastic spoon into the ashes and bring out roughly half a teaspoon. I sprinkle it in with the glitter and glue and mix it all together. After finding a tiny paint brush in the craft bucket, I dip it into the mixture. This has to be flawless. I test out the letter M on a scrap piece of paper. It's a perfect consistency.

"Ring around the rosy, a pocketful of posies. Ashes, ashes, we all fall down." As I sing, I scrawl *Old Mommy* above her photo in ashy-gold glitter glue.

When I'm done, I hold it up and stare at it in admiration. I show it to New Mommy. "I love this scrapbook. Thank you so much."

She doesn't say a word.

I nod to the box with Old Mommy's ashes. "Please put that somewhere where I can easily get to it."

Slowly, Daddy moves to tape the box back together.

With the scrapbook open to dry, I work at cleaning up my mess. New Mommy doesn't help me. She quietly watches me.

The oven timer dings indicating the brownies are done, but New Mommy doesn't move.

I walk over, take the brownies out, and turn the oven off.

Leaving the scrapbook open on the table to dry, I give them both a hug. "I love it here so much." Then, I take my sewing box and I go up to my bedroom to feed M&M New Mommy's diamond earrings.

That night, she comes into our room and takes Nathan with her. I suck my thumb and wait for them to return, but they never do.

Did she forget she was supposed to read me a bedtime story?

26

The next morning, I wake up before everybody else. A quick peek in M&M's food bowl shows me that he ate last night's treat.

Nathan's right. He's not a picky guinea pig.

After a quick trip to the bathroom, I tread the stairs down to the great room to check on my scrapbook. The sun hasn't risen yet and I pause at the giant windows to admire the dense fog hanging over the valley.

The moon barely glows through the haze. A thick quietness clings to the air that only comes at this time of the morning. It was Old Mommy's favorite part of the day. She loved sitting on the front steps, wrapped in a blanket, watching the night transition to day. I loved the mornings that I woke early enough to join her.

A sad smile curves my face. I can almost smell the tea she used to cradle in her hands. I can almost hear her raspy but gentle voice as she told me, "Good morning, my love."

I'm turning away from the windows when I see New Mommy sitting on the porch swing wrapped in a blanket and cradling a mug.

Heaviness pushes in on my chest and tears heat my eyes. I'm full-on crying by the time I put a coat and shoes on and walk out the side door.

New Mommy glances up from the end of the porch. "Francis, what's wrong?"

The sob comes so deep I can't even talk.

"Oh, my gosh." She puts the mug down and opens the blanket. "Come here."

My feet drag across the wooden planked porch. I barely make it. My body collapses against her.

"Sh. Sh." She holds me tight, rocking me, and I cry hard. It comes from deep in. It wracks my guts and rumbles my chest. I can't control it.

"I miss her so much," I sob.

"I know. Sh. Sh. It's okay." She kisses the top of my head and rocks me.

I cry, and I cry. My body heaves with the release. Snot trails from my nose. Tears push from my eyes. Just when I think they're subsiding, it starts again. I'm not sure how long I cry, but when I'm done, I lay limp against New Mommy. I'm exhausted.

Quietly, she continues holding and rocking me with the swaying of the porch swing. Eventually, I open my eyes, and I stare out across the valley as the moon and sun greet each other.

I'm warm and safe.

"Did you cry when you lost your husband and daughter?"

She pauses the swing for a second. "How do you know about my daughter?"

"Daniel told me."

The swing starts back up. "Yes, I cried hard."

"Like I just did?"

"Yes."

"Do you think crying helps?"

"Yes, I do. It's important to grieve."

"Last year Mommy cried hard when she lost Petra."

"Who's Petra?"

I pause. What's the best way to describe Petra? "I guess you could say she was Mommy's pet. I never liked her. I didn't cry when she died. Is that bad?"

"Of course not."

"That's good to know."

A few moments pass, and we continue swinging. I love New Mommy's hug. It feels genuine, like a hug she'd give Daniel or Nathan. I want to get more comfortable, but I'm afraid she'll stop holding me.

"You buried your husband and your daughter just down the hill. Do you think it helps to have them near?"

Again, the swing pauses. "I don't know. It was the best decision at the time." She breathes in deeply. "I just realized Rachelle's ashes are very much like my graves. You want her near, but you're not sure how to do that."

I nod. "Do you have any ideas?"

The swing starts back up. "I don't think keeping her in a box is the answer. Why don't we research some ideas? We can scatter her ashes somewhere. Turn them into jewelry. To be honest, I'm not sure of all the options."

She points down the valley in the direction of the graves. "Or plant them with a tree. We did that with a magnolia. You can't see it from here. It's too tiny. But one day it will be huge."

"I read that some people put them into a painting."

"Is that why you did that last night with the scrapbook?"

I nod.

"Oh." She breathes out. "That makes sense."

With a sigh, I get more comfortable and she lets me. We don't talk after that. We simply hug and swing and watch the sun gradually rise to warm the morning.

Eventually, everyone wakes up and our routine begins. But, unlike the other mornings, this time when New Mommy tells me goodbye, she hugs me for real.

27

I 've been running on a high, as Old Mommy used to say, since my time this morning with New Mommy. Heck, it didn't even bother me when someone at lunch "accidentally" tipped my milk over and it ran all down my new blue sweater and jeans. I simply asked to go to the bathroom, and I cleaned up.

Now it's recess and kids pour from the side door, eager to get outside and play. All around me I'm jostled, and I clutch my black and silver striped notebook to my chest. I've only been writing in it a couple of days, but it's full of observations and thoughts, ideas, and plans.

Private things.

A girl pushes past me, bumping me into another kid.

"Hey, watch it." The kid shoves me, and I lose my balance, falling backward into Maia.

"Get away from me, you creep!" She shoves me, too, and the spiral pad flies from my hands.

Kids laugh.

I scramble across the frozen grass for my notebook, but someone steps on it as they sprint past. My fingers connect with the spiral just as someone else kicks it away.

More laughter.

A hand reaches down to grab it, and I glance up to see Maia holding it. I climb to my feet.

She starts to hand it to me and on second thought stops.

"Give it to me." I hold a hand out.

"What are you always writing?"

"None of your business." I reach for it.

She tosses it over my head and a boy catches it. Anger fires through me, and I turn on him. It's Chris, the biggest kid in my class.

Anger is a useless reaction, Old Mommy used to say. I take a deep breath. "May I please have my notebook?"

Chris hesitates, then with a shrug, he holds the journal out for me. I step forward to take it and he throws it straight up into the air.

I watch it go up, pause midair, and then fall back to the ground. I grab for it at the same time Chris does. We yank in opposite directions and a few pages rip free.

A gust of winter wind kicks in, and the paper flies.

Maia laughs.

Chris laughs.

A few other kids laugh.

I scramble over the grass, desperately scooping up my thoughts.

More kids move in, looking, snickering.

On all fours I crawl as fast as I can, picking up the torn pages. I'm about to get the last one when a hand reaches down and grabs it.

It's Chris. "I love Maia's red hair," he loudly reads. "It reminds me of Mommy's hair. I want to wrap myself in it and—"

With a scream, I launch myself into Chris, and I knock him to the ground. I claw at his face, shrieking. "You're not good. You're bad. You're very bad!"

Chris rolls around underneath me, finally shoving me away. He clambers to his feet, his eyes wide. Blood slowly emerges from a scratch mark.

"What's going on here?" Mrs. Espy runs over.

Everyone around me falls silent.

I clutch the torn pages to my chest, and I cry as I glare at all the kids staring at me. "Dr. Dixon said you were good kids. You're not. You're bad. You're very bad. You should be ashamed of yourselves."

∼

"WE HAVE A NO-TOLERANCE policy in this school," the principal says, looking sternly at first Chris and then me.

Calmly I say, "I apologize."

"That's not good enough," Chris' Mom snaps. "Look at my son's face!"

His face has one tiny Band-Aid over an even tinier scratch. I could've and would've, done so much worse.

"Your son was teasing my son." Daddy nods to the striped notebook laying in my lap, now with the torn pages shoved back in. "That's my son's personal property, and yours ripped it."

"I did not," Chris grumbles.

The principal holds up a hand. "Any kind of physical altercation earns an automatic suspension. Given this—"

"If I may?" I sit up in my chair. "This whole thing has been a misunderstanding. You see, I dropped the notebook. Chris bent to pick it up at the same time I did. We both lost our balance, causing a few papers to rip. My fingernail inadvertently scratched his cheek. It was an accident." I look at Chris. "Right?"

"Uh...yeah, what he said."

"Chris was only trying to help," I say. "You don't need to be worried. Nothing like this will ever happen again. I promise."

His mom just looks at me.

I maintain a pleasant expression because Chris *will* pay for this.

Just wait.

28

After school Daddy and I sit in the bleachers watching Nathan do gymnastics. After this, we'll pick Daniel up from football and go home.

I draw a line under my one-step equation, write x = 5, and then close my math homework.

Daddy glances over. "Want me to check it?"

"Sure." I give him the math workbook, and he spends a moment double-checking my answers. He hands it back. "Perfect."

"Thanks."

"Are you sure Chris wasn't mean to you?"

"I'm sure."

A few seconds of silence go by. "Anything you want to talk about in your notebook? I'm happy to read your passages or discuss whatever you would like. I know Dr. Dixon would be happy as well."

"My notebook is private."

"Yes, I'm just making sure you know I'm here if you want to talk about anything."

"I'm good."

We sit silently after that, watching Nathan. I think I might like to join gymnastics.

Eventually, class is over. We load up in the Jeep and drive to the football field for Daniel. From there, it's home.

As we near our road, Daddy puts his blinker on before pulling off the highway. A half-mile in he turns to begin the drive up the ridge to our home when Minnie comes around the side of her small cabin carrying Boots. She waves for us to stop and Daddy brakes.

Daniel sits in the front seat. He glances back at me, but I ignore him as I stare at Boots. Minnie draws closer to the Jeep, and as she does, the bandage around Boots' head becomes evident.

Rolling his window down, Daddy says, "Oh my God, Minnie. What happened?"

Dressed in a long sweater and mittens, she stops a few feet away from the Jeep. One-Eyed-Boots looks right at Daddy and hisses.

"Oh, stop it," Minnie says, rubbing his head. "Not entirely sure. The doctor thinks he took a pellet in the eye. Either way, I wanted to let you know I found him."

"Is he going to see out of that eye?" Daddy asks.

"No, it's been removed and stitched shut." She kisses Boots' head, and he hisses again at Daddy.

I'm sitting behind the driver's seat, and I roll my window down. One-Eyed-Boots makes eye contact with me. One beat goes by as he processes who I am, and then he burrows into Minnie's sweater to hide his face.

"Aw, it's okay." She snuggles him. "I've never seen him like this. He's so affectionate." She massages his neck. "Well, anyway, just wanted to let you know."

With another wave, she turns away.

I roll my window back up.

The Jeep pulls forward, continuing the climb up the ridge.

"What's a pellet?" Nathan asks.

"Buckshot. There are a lot of hunters in these mountains." Daddy shifts to a lower gear. "Maybe that pellet was a God send. He'll be better behaved and a better companion for Minnie."

"Sometimes a lesson needs to be learned," I say. "Now he knows not to stray far from home."

"Here's hoping," Daddy agrees, and Daniel once again looks over his shoulder at me.

29

The next afternoon we ride the bus home from school. I get another wink from Ms. Sally-Anne.

At home, Daddy tells us he has a couple more hours of work. Daniel heads to the fort, probably to smoke and look at naked women. I continue my cross-stitch project of Boots. Nathan disappears upstairs to watch cartoons.

I've been downstairs for about fifteen minutes or so when Nathan trudges the stairwell down to the first floor.

"Have you seen M&M?" he asks.

Yes. "No."

He takes a minute to look around the great room, peeking under couches and behind furniture. He even circles through the kitchen and opens a few of the lower cabinets.

"Did you leave his door open?" I ask.

"No, and even if I did, M&M never comes out on his own."

"Then why would he be downstairs?"

"I don't know." Nathan lets go of a sigh.

I push a black thread through, looping it under and back up. Normally, I'd be done by now, but I want to take my time with this one. "I heard Mommy's diamond earrings are missing too."

"What does that have to do with M&M?"

"You said he eats anything."

Nathan frowns.

I put my project aside. "Want to go outside and look?"

"Sure...I guess."

Daddy's still in the office with his door closed. I write a quick note and leave it on the kitchen island, so he knows where we are.

We slide into our jackets and gloves, Nathan puts a knit hat on, and out we go.

We spend the next hour looking around the yard. We walk the driveway down the ridge. We search the surrounding woods. I'm kind of tempted to show him where M&M is, but I'm more interested to see how this plays out.

I wonder when he'll start to smell.

Eventually, we circle back to find Daniel climbing down from the triangular-shaped fort.

"Have you seen M&M?" Nathan asks.

"No." Daniel walks off in the opposite direction. "It's logging day. I'll see you two later."

I look at Nathan. "Logging day?"

"Daniel likes to watch the logging trucks go by." Nathan walks toward the house. "I'm going to check inside again."

I follow Daniel.

"What are you doing?" he grumbles.

"I want to see the trucks too."

"Fine." He leads the way across the gravel driveway and cuts through the woods that border the back side of our property. We weave through thick pine trees dusted in snow.

About fifteen minutes later we emerge on a hill that overlooks a switchback road and a winding river. A red logging truck comes into view. It blows its horn as it begins navigating the zigzag narrow road.

Daniel sits on the edge of the overhang, dangling his feet over the side. Roughly twenty feet down is the road. A thick net covers the steep hill, keeping the loose dirt and rocks in place.

The semi-truck's gears grind, smoke billows from the exhaust, slowly it climbs.

The truck expertly makes it around the first two hairpin turns, gears grind again, it begins its descent. It passes right under us. The logs teeter back and forth. The truck disappears around the corner.

"Do they ever topple over?" I come closer to the edge.

He shrugs. "None that I've seen."

Another truck comes into view, this one blue.

We watch it repeat what the red one did, eventually passing under us and following the first around the bend.

Another truck comes into view.

I see why Daniel likes this. It's the suspense. Will they make it, or will they tip over? It's kind of like a game.

But, every good game needs obstacles, or what's the point?

As Daniel keeps watching I look down the overhang. On closer inspection, I now see the net only covers the bottom three-fourths. The top portion remains open to the elements. Curious, I use my shoe to toe a jagged rock, but it stays firmly in place.

The truck passes underneath us.

I look to the right, spying a watermelon size boulder a few yards away. It doesn't look like it's seated too firmly. Too bad I didn't think to bring a crow bar.

I walk over.

"Where are you going?" Daniel asks.

"Nowhere. Just walking the edge."

Another truck comes into view. Daniel turns away from me to watch.

I meander over and sit on the boulder. Daniel quickly glances at me before looking back at the truck. It blows its horn. I move back and forth on the large rock, finding it loose. I watch the truck take the first two turns. Two more and it'll be right under me. I move back and forth again, the boulder jostles underneath me. The truck's gears grind. It navigates the third switch back. Smoke shoots from the exhaust. I watch it carefully.

Five.

Four.

Three.

Two.

I stand up quickly, making sure to put all my weight into the movement. A hot thrill races through me as I shove the boulder with both my hands.

It topples over the hill and down, down, down to clear the net. It lands twenty feet below on the road and burst into fragmented rocks. The truck slams on its brakes. The back-end fishtails. The cab teeters. The tires squeal. The logs break free. They roll off the side, bumping into each other, and straight down into the river.

The truck jerks as it slides to a complete stop. The driver erupts from the cab. Another semi comes into view.

"Hey!" The driver angrily shouts, and I look down to see him glaring up at us.

I turn toward Daniel, but he's already running back into the woods.

I follow at a slower pace.

~

"THAT WASN'T FUNNY!" Daniel shouts at me when I catch up to him in the woods.

"You're right, it wasn't. I didn't mean to knock that boulder over."

He rounds on me. "Oh, bullshit. You did too!"

"Did you see me push it?" I blink.

"N-no, not exactly."

I keep walking. "Then there you have it."

He begins walking too.

"Besides, no one got hurt. The driver is fine."

"That's not the point."

"You have to admit, that was fun watching. It was like one of your video games but in real life."

"So, you did do it?"

"I didn't say that."

Daniel marches past me. "We have to tell Carter and Mom."

"Yeah, I guess. But imagine how much trouble we'll be in. Maybe it's best to keep this between us. I mean, again, no one got hurt."

Daniel comes to the edge of the woods. He stops and looks at me. "Let me guess, another secret."

I smile. "It's either that or get in trouble. Do you want to get in trouble?"

"No."

"Then, there you have it." I walk past him. "Come along, Daniel. Time to go inside."

30

That night I lay in the top bunk, sucking my thumb and listening to New Mommy read both of us a bedtime story. She's not laying with Nathan, but she's not with me either. She sits in a desk chair with her legs crossed quietly telling us the story.

The guinea pig's empty home takes up the corner.

"What if we can't find M&M?" Nathan had asked New Mommy and Daddy during dinner.

"Then we'll get a new one," Daddy had said.

"I don't want a new one," Nathan had mumbled.

I was glad to hear that response. Little Brother will be sad for a while. But eventually, he'll get over it. Plus, now that the rodent's gone, we can get rid of its house. I can put my bed over there versus on top of Nathan's. New Mommy can easily climb in with me then.

Gradually, her soft voice drifts away as Nathan's heavy breathing fills the room.

She closes the book and stands. I'm not ready for her to leave. I'm not asleep yet.

She kisses Nathan first and then smiles at me.

She turns to leave, and I slide my thumb from my mouth. "Is Daddy going to lick you again tonight?"

31

The next morning Daddy asks me to come into his office. He closes the door behind us, motioning for me to sit wherever I want.

There is a desk and chair, a drafting table and high stool, plus filing cabinets and shelves. I choose the high stool, and he sits in his desk chair.

Out in the great room, New Mommy's making breakfast for Nathan and Daniel. I can't believe it's Friday already. Tomorrow I will have been here for one whole week.

Leaning forward, Daddy clasps his fingers between his knees and he looks up at me on the high stool. "Tori told me what you said to her last night about...about..." He clears his throat. "About licking."

I nod.

"How do you know about that?"

"Because I saw you."

His face falls. "What? When?"

"A few nights ago. I came into your room, and I saw your head between her legs. You were making a licking noise, and she was moaning with climax."

He stares at me. "How do you know about climax?"

"Mommy."

"Rachelle told you about sex?"

I nod.

"You're ten."

"I know how old I am."

Blowing out a breath, he leans back in his chair. He stares at the ceiling.

"Mommy's climax sounded different, though."

His head jerks up. "*What*?"

"She sounded different. When she masturbated. That's when you—"

"I know what masturbation is." Daddy's face goes pale. I wait for him to say something more, but he doesn't.

"Daddy?" I prompt.

His voice comes hoarse. "When's the next time you talk with Dr. Dixon?"

"Tuesday."

Again, I wait for him to speak, but he doesn't.

"Is that it?" I ask.

Slowly, he nods.

"Okay." I jump down from the drafting stool and open the door. New Mommy looks up from where she stands at the kitchen island making breakfast. The smell of sausage hits me, and I smile as I skip over. "Can I have two patties? I'm particularly hungry this morning."

~

At eleven in the morning, my classmates rush outside for recess. I follow at a slower pace, carrying my spiral notebook, now with the torn pages taped in at the seam.

Chris comes up behind me. He whispers, "'It reminds me of Old Mommy's hair. I want to wrap myself in it and drink milk.'"

I stop walking. Chris pushes past me, laughing.

That's okay. We'll see who's laughing by the end of the day.

Sliding my gloves off, I tuck them in my jacket pockets. I find Mrs. Espy. "I forgot my gloves. May I go back in and get them?"

"Five minutes. Make it quick." She wears the classroom key around her neck, and she takes it off and hands it to me.

"Yes ma'am."

I cross over the frosty grass and walk back in the side door. A quick pace down the hall and to the left and I use the key to get back in. I go straight to the cubbies that line the back wall. The one labeled CHRIS sits upper right.

Taped to the wall above the cubbies is a comprehensive list of students and allergies. I have no allergies, so my name is not on that list. Chris' is though right next to the words CELERY, WHEAT, NUTS, MILK.

What a shame he has so many issues.

His blue lunchbox sits upright, and I slide it from the cubby. After opening it, I survey the items. There's a thermos, a gluten and dairy-free Lunchable, a Ziplock with baby carrots, a snack bag of dried fruit, another of crackers labeled, "made with coconut flower," and turkey jerky. He's a big kid. I'm sure he eats all of this food.

I unscrew the thermos and sniff. I sample a tiny bit. It's beef bone broth. An interesting thing to put in a lunchbox.

I don't bring my lunch. I eat from the cafeteria. But I guess when you have so many food allergies, bringing your lunch is the only option. Too bad for Chris because our school cafeteria has decent food. Today is beefaroni day.

My assigned cubby sits right in the middle. I take my hard-plastic case and unsnap it. Underneath my neatly lined selection of pencils, markers, erasers, and stickers sits the baggie full of celery seed. I took it from our kitchen days ago when I first saw the allergy poster taped to the wall.

I'm not entirely sure how much celery seed to use, but I sprinkle a liberal amount in the bone broth. I give it another quick taste to find it's a bit different but not so much that Chris will notice.

I repack his lunchbox exactly like I found it and position it in his cubby. I put my pencil case back as well. The empty baggie goes in my pocket to be disposed of outside. Our classroom has two doors—one at the front and one at the rear. It's as I'm wedging my gloves on that I see Nathan looking at me through the vertical strip of glass on the rear door.

I'm across the room in seconds and I yank it open. He jumps back.

"What are you doing on my side of the school?" I demand.

He holds up a hall pass and points to the classroom beside mine. "My teacher sent me to deliver a file to that teacher. That's my job this month. I'm the class runner."

I look up and down the hall to find it empty.

"I-I know this is your classroom," he says. "I peeked in to see."

"It's recess." I push him out of the way and close the door.

"What are you doing then?"

"I had to get my gloves. My teacher said I could." I show him the key for proof.

I start walking back the way I came with my hand firmly on his upper back. At the end of the hall, I turn toward the side door and on second thought I look back at Nathan. I'm not sure how much he saw, but his face says he saw something.

32

"I wish you could've seen it!" Daniel excitedly announces at dinner. "The kid was clutching his throat and gasping. He turned purple. They shoved one of those Epi-Pens into his leg. An ambulance arrived. The whole cafeteria saw. It was epic."

No, epic would have been if Chris died.

"Daniel." New Mommy shakes her head. "Don't be so excited about it. That poor kid could've died. Allergies are serious business. We're lucky none of us have them."

Daddy eats a bite of pork chop. "What kid is this?"

"It's Chris. That dude that was picking on Francis." Daniel looks at me. "Right, wasn't it Chris?"

"I never said he was picking on me." I dab the sides of my mouth with a napkin. "The whole thing with the notebook and me accidentally scratching him was a misunderstanding."

Nathan pauses with a fork to his mouth. He looks across the table at me. I return his look as I cut a piece of meat.

He wisely says nothing.

～

AFTER DINNER, I throw all my energy into Nathan. "Want to play *Sequence for Kids*?"

"Sure, I guess." He shrugs.

"Great!"

I grab the board game and take it up to our room. I spread it out on the carpeted floor. After dealing the cards I nod for him to go first.

With about as much enthusiasm as a kid eating liver, he places a green disc on the board and selects a replacement card.

"I love being brothers." I grin. "I never had one before."

He nods.

I place a red disc on the opposite corner, choose a replacement card, and he goes next. "It's been a good week, I think." I look around the room. "Did you ever share a room with Daniel?"

"He'd throw a giant fit if Mommy and Carter ever suggested it."

I frown. "I'm sorry. That's not very nice."

"I'm used to it." Nathan puts another green disc down and selects a card.

"What do you mean?"

"Nothing, I guess. Most of the time I get on his nerves. At least that's what he says."

I take my turn, putting another red disc down. "Well, you don't get on my nerves. If anyone gets on my nerves, it's Daniel. Not you."

Nathan looks up at me. "Really?"

I grin. "For sure. It's you and me against Daniel," I say in a joking voice, though I like that idea very much.

Nathan finally smiles. He takes another turn.

"Dude," I mimic Daniel, and laughter flickers through Nathan's eyes.

The next few rounds of play go by and with each one, Nathan gradually eases back into comfort with me. I play all over the board, giving him lots of open spaces. After a few minutes I say, "Can I tell you a secret? Just between two brothers?"

"Okay."

"That boy Chris doesn't like me. He bullies me and calls me bad names. He picks on me. He's so big, he scares me." I nibble my bottom lip, faking the fear. "I don't know what to do. I lied to the principal and Daddy. I told them Chris wasn't being mean to me because I'm afraid of what he'll do if I tell the truth."

Nathan stops playing the game. "Did you make Chris sick?"

"No, of course not." I work up tears, surprised how easy they come. "I'd never purposefully hurt anybody. Please don't tell that I lied about Chris bullying me. Will you be a good brother and keep my secret?"

He puts his cards down and hugs me. "Of course, I will. But if he keeps being mean to you, you have to tell. Promise?"

"I promise." With a smirk, I squeeze him tight. "Thank you for the advice. I love you, Little Brother."

"I love you, too."

He sits back and picks his cards up. One more turn and he grins. "Sequence!"

Laughing, I toss my hand at him. "No way!"

He giggles.

Daniel walks through the open door. He looks between us as our laughter dies away. "What are you two doing?"

"Playing Sequence," I say. "Duh!"

Nathan giggles.

Daniel scowls. "Can I play?"

I look at Nathan. "What do you think?"

"Hm." Nathan taps his chin. "Maybe if you said please," he teases.

"Whatever." Daniel walks out.

"Whatever," I mimic, and Nathan giggles again.

33

The next morning, Nathan and I sit side-by-side at the kitchen island eating cereal for breakfast. Daddy's busy in the kitchen wiping and re-wiping a counter. New Mommy is drinking coffee and staring at Nathan with an intense focus like she needs to say something but doesn't know how.

Nathan eats his last bite and Daddy clears his bowl.

"I love Saturday," Nathan announces. He looks at me. "Want to go outside and play?"

New Mommy clears her throat. "Nathan, we want to chat with you."

"Okay."

Daddy puts the rag down and turns to stand beside New Mommy. He looks at her, Nathan, me, then back to Nathan. "Buddy, we found M&M."

I take another bite of cereal. *Here we go.*

"Really?" Nathan brightens. "Where is he?"

New Mommy and Daddy exchange another look.

My eyes drift over to the laundry room.

She says, "Sweetheart, we found him behind the dryer." She puts her coffee down and walks around the island to Nathan. "He's not alive anymore."

"What?" Tears pool in Nathan's eyes. "What do you mean?"

"He crawled behind, and he couldn't get back out." She hugs him. "I'm so sorry."

Well, I shoved him back there, but whatever.

Nathan sobs. "No, Mommy, no."

She holds him tight, rocking him while he cries.

I finish my cereal, listening to him sob. Maybe I should tell him M&M was already dead. He didn't feel any pain back behind that dryer. But if I tell Nathan that, then I'll have to detail how I killed M&M, and I don't want to. I like having that secret.

Instead, I say, "I'm sorry, Nathan." Because that's what people say when something dies.

Little Brother continues crying, and I look at Daddy to see tears cloud his eyes.

Daniel treads the stairs down to the great room, coming to a stop when he sees what's going on. "Who died?" he jokes.

I almost laugh. *Good one, Daniel.*

Nathan jerks away from New Mommy. He swivels around on his chair and glares. "I hate you!" he shouts.

Daddy holds a hand up. "Daniel, we found M&M." He shakes his head.

"Oh." Daniel cringes.

Crying, Nathan turns back to hug New Mommy. Daniel awkwardly approaches.

"Where did you find him?" he whispers to Daddy, and he tells him.

"How did he get in the laundry room?" Daniel asks.

"I don't know," Daddy mumbles, and Daniel looks right at me.

I ignore him.

A few quiet moments go by while Nathan cries himself out.

I look between Daddy and New Mommy, excited for what I'm about to suggest. I hope they say yes. "We should bury M&M with the others."

~

AT TWO IN the afternoon when everyone is ready, the five of us leave the house and walk the front yard down the hill to the graves.

Finally, I get to see them up close and personal. It's not like I couldn't come down here by myself, but I wanted to wait.

I have questions.

Behind us, the house stands warm and welcoming. In front, the valley softly rolls down and then back up. Mountains bump the horizon.

Two gray marble slabs mark John and Samantha's lives. On each slab lay bundled flowers that look to be days old. In between the two, a magnolia sapling grows. That's the one New Mommy told me about.

Kneeling, she picks the old flowers up and replaces them with two new bundles. Nathan cradles a tiny wood casket that Daddy made. Daniel digs a small grave to the left of the marble slab labeled JOHN LAMBERT.

Daddy begins reading something he printed off the internet. "There is a bridge connecting Heaven and Earth. It is called the Rainbow Bridge because of its many colors. Just this side of the Rainbow Bridge there is a land of meadows, and hills and valleys with lush green grass. When a beloved pet dies…"

Idly I listen as I study the graves. "Are their ashes in there or bodies?"

Abruptly Daddy stops.

New Mommy stares at me.

Daniel glares.

Nathan tightens the hold on M&M's casket.

"They both were cremated," New Mommy whispers. "Their ashes are buried here, not their bodies."

I nod.

Daddy starts back up, "The animals are happy and content, except for one small thing. They each miss someone very special to them, who had to be left beh—"

"Was there an autopsy done?"

Daddy sighs. "No."

"We should probably do one on M&M. Don't you want to know what's in his stomach? You might be surprised." Or maybe M&M pooped out the diamond earrings. I should've thought to check his litter.

New Mommy's stare intensifies.

Daniel narrows his eyes, silently threatening.

Nathan begins to cry.

Daddy shoots me a warning glare, but I'm not sure what he's warning me about. I'm just asking questions.

He continues, "They run and play together until the day comes when one of them suddenly stops playing and looks off into the distance. The nose twitches. The ears—"

"When Mommy buried Petra, she buried her body, just like we're burying M&M's body. But Mommy was cremated, like John and Samantha. They don't have bodies anymore."

"Petra?" Daddy asks.

"Mommy's pet. If I were to dig these graves up, what would I find?" I look at him. "Just the ashes or a box with the ashes?"

New Mommy gasps.

Nathan's cries turn to choking sobs.

Daniel throws the shovel down and comes at me.

Daddy steps between us. "Francis, I know you don't realize this, but you are being disrespectful. This is sacred ground to this family. You need to be quiet and reverent. Stop asking questions. If you have anything else to ask, come to me later. Do you understand?"

"Yes."

Daddy continues reading the rest of whatever it is he printed. Nathan places the small casket into the ground. Daniel covers it up with dirt and then Nathan lays a handful of carrots on top. His version of flowers, I suppose.

New Mommy hugs him, and the four of them turn away to walk back to the house. From my coat pocket, I take out the mini-Tupperware that I filled with Old Mommy's ashes. I wedge the lid off and I sprinkle her over all three graves.

New Mommy knocks the container from my hand. She grabs my upper arm and shakes me. "What do you think you're doing?"

I blink. "Adding Mommy to the mix. Why?"

34

The rest of the weekend, New Mommy doesn't speak to me, doesn't talk to me, doesn't even look at me.

She's mad.

But she's the one who said *We can scatter the ashes somewhere.* What's wrong with putting some on John and Samantha? Aren't we all one big family?

On Monday Daddy gets Nathan and Daniel early from school for simultaneous dentist appointments. I'm about to climb on Ms. Sally-Anne's bus home when a teacher pulls me from the line. "Your mom is here."

I find her SUV parked midway with all the other parents waiting to pick up their kids. With a big smile, I climb in the back. I bet she's here so we can spend time together. She's sorry for giving me the silent treatment. I knew she'd come around.

After I close the back door, she says, "Last minute change. Minnie can't see you home from the bus stop and Carter's stuck at the dentist with Daniel and Nathan. Therefore, I'm here." Without looking at me, she puts the SUV in gear. "I have to run errands."

"Okay, Mommy."

Her jaw tightens. I'm beginning to realize she does that when she's irritated. I wonder if she knows it's not good to clench your teeth.

I wouldn't want her to get dental damage.

We go to the bank first where she takes money from the ATM. Next, we go to a dry cleaner where she drops off clothes and picks some up. After that, it's the pharmacy for a prescription, and then comes the grocery.

She parks in the lot. I unbuckle my seatbelt and climb out. She hesitates as if she's considering telling me to wait. But I don't give her a chance, I lead the way into the grocery.

She grabs a cart and starts in the produce aisle.

I follow.

After referencing a list, she chooses broccoli, spinach, and apples.

I hold up a pineapple. "Can I have this?"

"No."

She moves on to bread, quickly finding the Hawaiian loaf that Nathan likes.

I hold up sourdough. "Can I have this?"

"No."

She rounds the corner to the cereal aisle. She selects honey oats —Daniel's favorite—and puts the box in the cart.

I hold up chocolate puffs. "Can I have this?"

"No."

Another quick look at the list. She moves onto the chip aisle, putting mini pretzels—her favorite—in the cart.

I hold up salt and vinegar. "Can I have this?"

"No."

She turns the corner where the candy is, finding Twizzlers— Daddy's favorite.

I select Reese's Pieces. "Can I have this?"

"No."

I follow her around to canned goods. Again, she reviews the list, selecting several things—chili, mushrooms, black beans...

I find a glass container of artichokes. "Can I have this?"

"No."

Fine. I drop it to the ground. It shatters. "Oops."

She whips around. A girl stocking shelves at the end of the aisle says, "Don't worry, we'll clean it up."

"Sorry," New Mommy calls out before glaring at me.

Inside, I sneer.

"Be careful," she warns.

I nod, already planning the next item.

We round to the spaghetti aisle. I don't bother asking. I pick out the biggest glass jar of chunky tomato I can find, and I lob it into the air. It lands with a loud resounding crack. Glass shatters and red sauce splatters across the floor, the shelves, me, New Mommy.

"Oops."

"Francis!"

The same stock girl comes running around the corner.

New Mommy grips my upper arm and shakes me, just like she did at the graves. "What is wrong with you?"

Loudly, I say. "Mommy, you're hurting me!"

She releases me and steps back, glancing around to see if anyone heard.

I walk off. "At least now I know what it takes for you to pay attention to me."

35

L ater at dinner, the tension between me and New Mommy is thicker than ever.

I poke at my beef and broccoli as I listen to Nathan talk about today's show and tell. "I couldn't believe it when her dad walked in carrying a gigantic white snake around his neck!"

"You hate snakes," Daddy says.

"I know! He walked up and down the aisles, so we could pet it. I was so scared I asked my teacher to leave. She let me stand in the hall."

"Were you the only one?" New Mommy asks.

"No, there were a few of us too afraid."

New Mommy looks at Daddy. "I'm surprised the school let him bring that in."

"Mm," Daddy agrees. He looks at Daniel. "How's your mouth feeling?"

He frowns. "I hate getting my teeth cleaned. It's not supposed to hurt, is it?"

"Not particularly," New Mommy says. She sips her iced tea. "I'll let the hygienist know for next time. They have a numbing gel that they can put on your gums."

My new family continues eating and talking. No one asks me how my day was. With a sigh, I poke at my food. Maybe if I threw it against the wall, they'd notice me. "May I be excused?"

"No," New Mommy says just as Daddy replies, "You haven't eaten anything."

"No," New Mommy repeats. "You don't pull a temper tantrum at the grocery and then come home and refuse to eat. Our family doesn't work that way."

Daddy looks between us. "What happened at the grocery?"

"Francis purposefully threw two glass jars on the floor. He made a mess, and he embarrassed me."

"I told you, I just wanted you to pay attention to me," I quietly say.

"That's not what you said. You said, 'At least now I know what it takes for you to pay attention to me.' That's manipulative and unacceptable. That's not the way to get my attention." She nods to my plate. "Now, eat."

"No, thank you." I push the food away. "I want to be excused. Now."

"No."

I glare at New Mommy, ready to throw my food at her and not the wall.

She glares right back.

"Fine," Daddy sighs. "You can get up."

~

THAT NIGHT my new parents argue so loudly that Nathan crawls into bed with me. I hug him the whole night. It's the best night's sleep I've had since finding Old Mommy dead in her bed.

36

"Would you like to share your notebook with me?" Dr. Dixon asks the following day.

"No, Daddy said it's private."

"It is private, but you're welcome to share it any time you'd like. No judgment."

Today Dr. Dixon wears a purple bowtie. I wear a yellow and white one. Mine is better than his, but I can't seem to stop staring at his. It's the wrong shade of purple and it gets on my nerves. So does his smile, which he's doing right now as he dunks a tea bag up and down in steamy water.

Would you like to share your notebook with me?

He asks me that every time I see him, even out in the halls. It annoys me. *He* annoys me. I wish Joanie White had his job. She'd do a lot better at it than he does. She wouldn't constantly ask to see my notebook.

"How are you doing at home?" he asks.

"Fine." I frown. "Why, did Mommy talk to you?"

"No, should she?"

In my head, I roll my eyes. This is another thing that annoys me. He answers questions with questions. Joanie White wouldn't do that.

"Not particularly," I say.

Loudly he sips his tea. The lippy sound grates my nerves.

"I've encouraged your parents to contact me if they have any questions. I'm also scheduled to sit down with them at the thirty-day mark. We can certainly meet before then if there's anything you want me to talk to them about."

This is news to me. "What do you mean you 'sit down' with them at the thirty-day mark?"

"We discuss your progress at school and home."

"Do you tell them what we talk about?"

"No. Your parents understand that confidentiality is key to us communicating." He takes his glasses off and cleans them. "Which I encourage you to do more of. You can trust me, Francis."

"I know," I say because it's what he wants to hear. "Does it go both ways? Do you tell me stuff?"

He slides his glasses back on. "Sometimes I might."

"Like?"

"Like, I grew up poor, but I went on to graduate with honors from a top university. Sometimes the way you're raised is motivation to be different."

Is he trying to tell me that I should change? Joanie White wouldn't tell me that. She likes me for exactly who I am. "I don't want to be different."

"Then be you." He gives me another annoying smile. "It's okay to be *exactly* who you are."

Well, that's good to know.

"Back to your parents. Your dad said you walked in on him and Tori having a private moment. Would you like to talk about that? How did it make you feel?"

It makes me feel like I want to jab his eye out.

"I need to go to the bathroom," I say.

"Oh sure."

I leave, fake diarrhea, and I don't return.

37

That afternoon, Daddy picks us up from the bus stop. I get another wink and smile from Ms. Sally Anne.

As we pass Minnie's house, I say, "Will you stop? I want to give Minnie the cross-stitch of Boots that I made."

Daddy puts the Jeep in park. I'd wrapped her present in a striped cloth and put it in my bookbag. I find it now and climb from the back seat. It only takes me a second to run across her yard and leave it at her front door.

With a big grin, I jump back into the Jeep. It's too bad I won't be there to see her face when she opens it. I hope she notices the details and realizes I'm the reason why Boots is better behaved now.

When we get up to the house, Daddy makes us a snack of cheese and crackers. Daniel goes to the fort, probably to smoke and look at naked women again. Nathan and I try to build a snowman but too much has melted, and our snowman ends up looking dirty and lopsided.

"Hide and seek?" Nathan suggests.

"Good idea. You hide. I'll seek."

Giggling, he takes off running. I cheat as I count loudly and watch where he goes. "One, two, three…"

I used to play hide and seek with Old Mommy.

Here kitty, kitty, kitty...

Nathan races under the house where Daddy and New Mommy park their cars. Other than the Jeep and tool shed, there is no place to hide under there. This will be easy.

When I'm done counting, I walk slowly toward the parking area. I check under the Jeep and inside it as well, and then I go straight to the shed with the tools. This must be where Daddy used to keep Old Mommy's ashes.

Now she's inside and warm.

I open the door and Nathan leaps out. "Boo!"

He runs past me, and I stand unmoving staring at a dog cage in the back corner.

"What are you doing?" Nathan comes back.

"Where did that come from?" I point.

"Oh, we used to have a lab. It died. Mommy and Carter said we'd get another. We just haven't yet. Do you like dogs?"

I walk over and lift the corner, finding it lighter than our other one.

"What are you doing?" Nathan asks.

"Nothing." I turn away. "I'm going inside to do homework."

$\sim$

THE SMELL of dinner permeates the air. We sit down for tacos. Even though I heard them arguing last night, Daddy and New Mommy seem okay.

New Mommy even asks me a question, "Our town has a winter carnival every year. We go as a family. Does that sound like fun? It's coming up this weekend."

I shrug, thinking about the cage as I've been doing since coming inside.

Dinner continues.

Daniel describes in too much detail how he won today's relay race during gym class.

Nathan tells everyone about this kid at lunch who laughed so hard corn blew from his nose.

The family laughs.

Daddy says, "Francis, that was really sweet of you to give Minnie that present. I would've loved to see the final product."

I shrug again.

"May I be excused?" I ask, and unlike last night, New Mommy doesn't object.

In my room, I sit on the floor, staring at M&M's play area. That'd be a good place to put the dog cage.

"Francis?" Softly, Daddy knocks on the door as he steps inside. "You okay?"

"Can we pack up M&M's area and put the dog cage there?"

Daddy doesn't respond.

I look up at him. "The cage in the tool shed. Can we put it there?"

"Wh-why—" He clears his throat. "Why do you want to do that?"

"I want to put Mommy's ashes in it." She'd like that. I go back to looking at the area. "Or we could put my bed there, I guess." It is what I wanted to do originally.

He jumps at that. "Yes, let's do that. We'll put your bed there."

We work together, taking the guinea pig area apart and packing the pieces into a box. New Mommy comes in to see what we're doing. Daddy tells her, and before she has a chance to respond he says, "Can you please talk to Nathan?"

With a nod, she quietly leaves the room.

It takes us about an hour to complete the transition.

Halfway through, Daddy asks, "Did you talk to Dr. Dixon today?"

"Not really. He had a stomach issue and kept going to the bathroom."

"Oh."

We don't say anything after that, and when we're done, Nathan comes in. He takes in the new configuration. "I like it," he says.

After that, it's bath time and then bedtime.

Daddy kisses me goodnight. New Mommy comes in to snuggle with Nathan and read a bedtime story. I suck my thumb and listen.

But this time when she finishes and Nathan's breathing heavy with sleep, she steps across the room to my bed and sits on the edge. My heart pauses. I can't believe it. Is she going to read to me too?

A small smile touches her lips. "What do you say you and me start over? I think we've gotten off on the wrong foot. I want us to be a family. I want us to love each other."

"I do love you," I say around my thumb.

"I know you do."

I wait for her to say she loves me back, but she doesn't.

"How about I read you a story?" She holds up the book she just read to Nathan. "This one or any of the others."

"I don't care." I scoot over, glad to have my bed on the floor. Now she doesn't have to climb a ladder to get to me. "That one's fine."

Carefully, she moves alongside me, propping herself up against the headboard. She doesn't open an arm for me, but I still snuggle in. As she flips the front cover of the picture book, I start sucking my thumb again.

Quietly, she reads, and I follow the words with her soft tone.

She turns a page, looking down at me.

I look back.

Her voice continues, melodic with rhyming words.

My eyes grow heavy with sleep.

She turns another page.

With a sigh, I snuggle further into her side as I slide my thumb from my mouth.

She turns another page, softly speaking.

I inhale slowly, drawing in her flowery scent. New, but also familiar.

Her voice lowers, sensing my sleepiness.

I nestle in.

She wears a white robe over her pajamas and my hand slides inside searching for her nipple.

She leaps from the bed. "What are you doing?"

"Having my nightly milk."

PART III

Tori

38

I pace the master bedroom. Every muscle in my body clenches tight. "Nightly milk, Carter? What the hell? Was Rachelle actively breastfeeding him?"

"Lower your voice." Carter casts a nervous glance toward the closed bedroom door.

"I want to put a nanny cam in their room," I say.

"You want to, *what?*"

I stop pacing. "You have a problem with that?"

"I'm not doing that. I'm not spying on my son. It's creepy and it goes against everything Dr. Dixon said."

I stare at my husband sitting on the bed. I hate that Francis looks just like him. "Oh, I see. It's okay for *my* son Nathan to share a room with your son, who we barely know. What if Francis touches him?"

"Francis won't touch him, and I thought Nathan was *our* son."

"Have you signed the adoption papers?"

Silence.

"What?" I snap.

"I can't find them."

"Of course, you can't." I throw my hands up. "What about the private investigator?"

Again, silence.

I swallow a growl of frustration. "Let me guess, you never hired one."

"I haven't had the chance."

"I don't even know what to say to you right now. I bet you haven't started the plans to build on either, have you?"

"Yes, I've begun some preliminary plans. Christ, he's not even been here two whole weeks yet. Give me a break."

If it had been John, the plans would be done, a contractor would have been hired, and he sure as hell would've followed through with a private investigator.

"His pictures are gone," I say.

"What are you talking about?"

"The Polaroids hidden in his sewing box? They're gone."

"You searched his things?"

"Yes. Frankly, I'm surprised you didn't."

"I'm trying to respect his privacy. When I called Dr. Dixon to speak with him about Francis seeing us being intimate and of course our conversation later, Dixon said that boundaries were important. That when—"

"Boundaries? Francis tried to breastfeed!" I grab a blanket off the corner chair. I'm done with this conversation. "I'm sleeping in the TV room. I need time to think."

39

The next afternoon, I sit beside Carter in Dr. Dixon's office. On speaker is Joanie White, the social worker from Murfreesboro.

I organized this impromptu meeting. When I called Carter from work to tell him about it, I said, "You can come or not."

He sits silently beside me.

I didn't sleep last night. Instead, I made a list of concerns, and I tried to look at everything from Carter's point of view. I understand he's excited to have a biological son. I also think that's blinded him to the reality of this situation.

Logically, I comprehend I'm too close. Which is why I called this meeting with Dr. Dixon and Joanie White. I value the importance of a third-party opinion.

I take in a breath and tell myself to remain calm and focused. Yet, my insides have been permanently clenched since last night with Francis. No, that's not true. They've been clenched since the moment I found out about him.

"Thank you for seeing us on such short notice," I begin. "Francis has been with us ten days now and there are things I'm concerned about. Carter and I have talked, and we would welcome impartial input." I look over at Carter to see him staring blankly down at the speaker phone.

"Certainly," Joanie White says and Dr. Dixon nods.

"In the car the day we brought Francis home, he talked non-stop about medieval torture techniques. He seemed obsessed with it. Like he wanted to actually do it or see it. The following day our boys went up to the fort built in a tree. Our youngest, Nathan, fell because Francis 'lost hold' of him. Granted, Nathan was wearing a harness and Francis apologized but something seemed off about the whole thing. I think Francis pushed him on purpose."

Carter jumps to his defense. "Francis wouldn't do that."

I ignore him. "He's too affectionate. He's always hugging me or wanting to be hugged. It's very uncomfortable. He also calls me 'Mommy' instead of Tori and that seems odd to me as I've only known him a small amount of time. I bought him a scrapbook as a welcome gift. The first thing he did was mix Rachelle's ashes with glitter glue and he wrote 'Old Mommy' on the first page next to a photo of her. Speaking of photos, he has several Polaroid shots that he brought with him. We asked to see them, but he won't agree to it. I want to respect his privacy, but I also want to know what those pictures are."

"If you want to respect his privacy, why did you ask me to put up a nanny cam?" Carter interrupts.

I cut him a look, but he's still staring blankly down at the speaker phone.

I reference the list I brought. "We had a funeral for Nathan's guinea pig, which is another thing I'm concerned about. We found his guinea pig dead behind the dryer. How did it get there? He never leaves his home unless you make him. That aside, we buried him next to my husband and daughter. Francis was disrespectful during the ceremony. He wanted to know details about their bodies, and then he had the audacity to scatter Rachelle's ashes on top of my husband and daughter's graves. He's manipulative and he's sneaky. I don't trust him, and I've tried. We even had a bonding moment one morning on the porch swing. But the breaking point came last night."

Again, I glance over to Carter, and still, he won't look at me.

"I asked Francis if we could start over. I laid in bed with him to read him a story, careful of boundaries as Dr. Dixon said. Francis was sucking his thumb and then he tried to breastfeed. He said he wanted his 'nightly milk.'" I look at the speaker phone. "Joanie, you said Rachelle's neighbor mentioned that something weird was going on in that house. You also mentioned the dog cage. Do you have any follow-up on those things?"

"Regarding that." Carter clears his throat. "We have one in our tool shed that I forgot about. Francis found it. He asked if we could move it inside. He wants to put his mother's ashes in it."

"*What?*" I gasp. "You didn't tell me that."

"If I may?" Dr. Dixon shifts forward. "I've been chatting with Francis nearly every day. He is a very sweet and bright boy."

The words grate through me. Mrs. Buchanan said the same thing.

He continues, "He has been raised isolated from the world. He's both mature and childish at the same time. Rachelle gave him uncensored access to a wide range of topics. I'm not sure you're aware of this, but she had a complete set of Encyclopedias that he's read. If he had a question, she always answered it. Nothing was off-limits. They talked in great detail about everything. It's like he was her husband, not her son. That's the mature side of him. But he's still a ten-year-old boy. He wants a Mommy and a Daddy. He sucks his thumb. He wants love and affection. It doesn't surprise me that Rachelle still breastfed him. It's a big adjustment moving in with you, experiencing a healthy family environment, having modern things, coming to school, and being surrounded by boys and girls his age."

His response does not sit well with me. "Joanie?" I prompt.

"First, let me say that I hear you. I understand your point of view. I had a limited week with Francis. It's good to know he's been meeting with Dr. Dixon regularly. If I had to describe Francis I would say well-mannered, intelligent, and curious. I encourage you to respect his privacy. Trust goes both ways. So does communication. Don't assume anything. Talk to him and ask him questions. For example, if you want to know if he had something to do with the guinea pig, ask him.

But be prepared for the answer as it may not be what you want to hear. Let him talk to you as he wants. It's a good sign he's talking to you about his mother. That means he's comfortable with you. It's also a good sign he asked about the cage. Give him the space to be who he is while at the same time offering guidance as to what is acceptable. Like with breastfeeding. Don't make him feel that's a bad thing. Simply let him know it's not something you do. Francis comes from a unique situation. You may never know all that went on inside that trailer and you have to be okay with that."

Dr. Dixon says, "There is no question he has attachment and developmental issues."

"Agreed," Joanie says.

"What about his request to bring the dog cage inside?" Carter asks. "We used to keep it in the laundry room when we had our lab."

Dr. Dixon looks at the speaker phone. "I don't know if you agree, Joanie, but if Francis isn't scared of it, let him have access to the cage. Observe him with it. See what happens. Let him know it's temporary, though. Come up with a mutually agreed-upon time. Say six months. That way he knows and can prepare himself that it will be moved back into the shed."

I shift uncomfortably in my chair. I'm not okay with this. "How do we explain that to Nathan and Daniel?"

"Tell them you're cleaning out the shed," Joanie suggests, agreeing with Dr. Dixon's recommendation. "Speaking of the boys, how are they getting along with Francis? Children are a good judge of character."

"Nathan adores him," Carter is quick to say. "Daniel's indifferent, but he seems that way about a lot these days."

Dr. Dixon and Carter both look at me.

A beat of awkward silence goes by. "I agree with what Carter just said."

Dr. Dixon says, "You went into his room last night to turn a corner. To start fresh. Why don't you do that? Draw a line and move forward. Don't get hung up on the past ten days. Make a new plan."

"I'd like that," Carter says.

"Okay." I nod.

But my new plan involves hiring a private investigator.

~

OUTSIDE THE SCHOOL, Carter walks me to my SUV. He opens the door for me. We stand silently staring at each other. He opens his mouth to say something but stops. I start to say something, but I stop too.

My lips press to a tight line.

We're supposed to be a team. We're supposed to have each other's backs. If Carter were John, it wouldn't be this way. John would be on my side no matter what. We would've gone in that meeting with the same concerns. He would've already signed the papers to adopt Nathan and Daniel. He would've agreed to a nanny cam. He would've been right there beside me trying to find the Polaroids.

And John certainly wouldn't have sat sulking and staring at the speaker phone.

"I'll see you later," I say, turning away.

"Yep."

I climb in my SUV and drive off, leaving Carter standing in the school parking lot watching my departure.

It takes me fifteen minutes to navigate town back to my office.

Once inside, I close my office door, and I sit on the couch in the corner. I don't even take my coat and gloves off or put my purse down. That's when I realize I'm shaking and my breaths come too quick and shallow.

Sliding the purse from my shoulder, I dig around inside, finding my anxiety pills. I swallow one with water and consider taking two. I hate that I'm relying on these again. I was doing so well.

Until Francis' arrival.

The pill kicks in quickly, giving me clarity and steadying my nerves.

Finally, I slide my gloves off, and I find my phone. Pulling up my contacts, I search for the P.I. our firm uses. I dial her number. She answers on the second ring.

I stay on the couch as I talk, giving her every detail of the past ten days. It takes me twenty minutes while she listens and jots notes.

"You've called the right person," she assures me. "I'll begin looking into this today."

We hang up, and I breathe deeply. It's the first real breath I've taken since Carter told me about Francis.

I finally feel in control.

40

That night after dinner, I handle putting my boys to bed while Carter and Francis bring the cage up from the tool shed and put it in the laundry room.

It only takes one book and Nathan falls asleep. Luckily, Francis is still downstairs with Carter and I don't have to read him a story.

In the master bedroom, I cross over to the closet, and I take down the box of Samantha's things.

One by one I lift out the items, carefully laying them on the bed.

There's the yellow outfit that she was supposed to wear on the way home from the hospital.

The crocheted pink and green blanket Minnie made for her.

The sterling silver spoon John engraved with her name.

The watercolor Daniel did of our house with the sun shining brightly.

The *Gift From Above* poem that I printed and framed.

Even though the onesie doesn't smell like her, I still lift it to my nose and inhale.

Tears warm my eyes and I cradle the fabric to my chest and rock it.

I cried in the weeks and months after coming home with just

Nathan. I cried while I bathed him. While I changed him. While I fed him. While I read to him and pushed him in the stroller and played with him.

It's something I deeply regret. I hate his first memories are of me crying. It shouldn't be that way.

The door opens. Carter quietly walks in. He pauses in the doorway to survey me on the bed surrounded by Samantha's things.

Normally, I hide my grief from him. I'm quick to dry my tears or push the sadness away. I never want Carter to feel uncomfortable or at a loss. I don't want him to feel responsible for repairing my broken heart.

Marrying me was a lot to take on. I know this. I come with so much baggage. Not only the loss of my daughter, but also the death of my husband, and two very much alive and healthy boys to raise.

Yes, I'm an expert at putting on a brave face for Carter. But this time I don't move to pack up Samantha's things. I give fully into the grief, crying hard into the onesie.

I never hid my feelings from John. He saw every side of me. John was strong that way.

Carter closes the door. He crawls in bed behind me, and he hugs me just like I'm hugging the onesie.

It reminds me of the way John used to console me, and that makes me cry even harder.

I miss John.

But as I do every day, I pretend my current husband is my dead one as I melt into his embrace.

41

The next morning, I peek into the laundry room. As expected, the cage sits there. Inside Francis placed the box with Rachelle's ashes. On top of the box sits an old baby rattle that I remember seeing in his things.

I snap a quick picture before leaving.

In my SUV, I navigate the ridge down to the main road. At Minnie's driveway, I pull in and park. The text she sent this morning said, CAN YOU STOP BY FOR A SEC?

SURE, I had texted back.

I'm about to climb from my SUV when she steps through her front door wrapped in a red robe and wearing clogs for shoes.

With a smile and wave, she crosses over her frosty yard to the driver's side.

"Good morning," she says as I roll my window down. "Thanks for stopping by."

"Sure thing. What's up?"

"I'd like to get your take on something." From the deep pocket of her robe, she takes out a six-by-six-inch framed object. "Francis left this on my front porch." She hands it to me.

The cross-stitched canvas depicts a detailed rendering of Boots sitting in a tree staring straight ahead. A red cross-haired bullseye has been sewn over his perfectly intact left green eye.

I sigh, already reaching for my phone. "Do you mind if I take a picture of this?"

"You can have it if you want it. It unsettles me."

"Understandably." I place the canvas in my purse, making a mental note to send a photo of it, along with the one I just took in the laundry room, to the P.I. "How did Francis know it was the left eye?"

"I saw the boys with Carter after school. I was carrying Boots. There was a bandage over his left eye. I told them the vet likely said it was a pellet of some sort."

"Hence the bullseye."

A bit of frigid air kicks in, picking at Minnie's long gray hair and sending the scent of coconut through the air. She takes a black band off her wrist and quickly gathers it into a side ponytail. "I really hate asking this question..."

"It's okay. Go ahead."

"Daniel has that BB gun. Have they been shooting it recently?" She shifts uncomfortably from one foot to the next. "I would understand if an accident happened and they were scared to tell me."

Carter did mention that Daniel and Francis had a good time shooting at targets in the yard. Mentally, I count back the days and my heart sinks as I realize the timing coincides with Boots missing, then showing up with a shot-out eye.

"Let me talk to the family," I say though I plan on talking to Daniel only. "I'm sorry about this."

"It's okay. Like I said, accidents happen, and Boots is fine. Actually, he's the most loving he's ever been with me. That aside, I would like to know, though."

"Of course."

We say goodbye, but I don't drive to the office, I drive straight to school.

I check Daniel out under the ruse of a doctor's appointment.

With a groan, he climbs into the passenger seat. "Another appointment? I just went to the dentist. What now?"

After closing the driver's door, I look at him. He's more and more like John every single day. My heart tugs.

"You don't have a doctor's appointment. I need to talk to you in private. By private I mean don't tell Carter or Nathan or Francis. Got it?"

He nods.

From my purse, I take out the canvas of Boots that Minnie gave me. I tell Daniel about my conversation with her ending with, "Did you boys accidentally shoot Boots?"

He barely looks at the canvas. "No."

I don't put it away. I leave it out for him to see. "Let me rephrase, did Francis accidentally shoot Boots?"

"No."

"Did he do it on purpose?"

"No! God, Mom, what the he—"

With a sigh, I pick the canvas of Boots up and put him back into my purse. "Is there anything you want to tell me about Francis?"

"No." He reaches for the door handle. "Is that it?"

"Daniel, look at me."

He does.

"If anything is going on, you need to tell me. You will not be in trouble."

He keeps looking at me.

"Okay?" I say.

"Whatever. Can I go?"

"Yes. Please remember this conversation is between you and me. Just tell the school I got the dates mixed up on your appointment."

"Yeah." He gets out, and I watch him walk across the lot and back into school.

I always knew when John was lying because he'd hold his eyes wide and gleaming, determined not to blink. He thought it made him look honest. It didn't. It made him look freakishly guilty. Granted his lies were harmless like, "Did you eat the last cookie?" and he'd reply with frozen open eyes, "Absolutely not."

Daniel does the same thing.

Which is how I know he just lied to me.

42

F or as long as I can remember, the local high school has hosted our town's winter carnival complete with rides and games, junk food and contests, silly shows, and music. For two nights the football field becomes an outdoor zone of fun.

Our family always goes on Friday night because that's the night the contortionist act performs, and we love to watch them.

Despite everything going on with Francis, I'm beyond excited about the annual outing.

We arrive just as night settles in and the lights flick on across the field. The rides and booths twinkle with red and yellow, purple and green. The sweet smell of funnel cake permeates the air. Music comes from all ends in disjointed carnival jingles.

With a deep breath in, I smile. I need this night. I can't wait to challenge Nathan at the Fish Cup booth.

I reach my hand back for my youngest, but he's already holding Francis' while he babbles on about the carnival. "Last year Daniel and I went in the funhouse. There's this mirror that makes you look as wide as a semi-truck! I can't wait for you to see the contortionist show. Last year Mommy rode the tilt-a-whirl and almost threw up. It was so funny. Oh, and we have to play that tossing game! I can't remember what it's called but they have the best prizes. Last year Daniel won a bubble gum machine. And face painting! Are you going to get your face painted?"

Francis laughs. "Yes!"

"Tell him about the pie in the face," Carter says.

"Oh, yeah!"

We take our place in line for tickets and Nathan keeps telling Francis about the carnival. Idly, I listen as I look around. In the line beside us stands a girl with long red hair and a big boy with a buzz cut. They're both surreptitiously looking at Francis.

Daniel nudges me, nodding their way. He whispers, "That's the boy that had the allergic reaction in the cafeteria." He lowers his voice even more. "And that's the girl Francis touched, ya know, her hair."

I nod.

Nathan keeps chatting. Francis keeps laughing.

We step up to the ticket booth.

Carter buys our usual amount and distributes them. Before I have a chance to give my warnings about staying together, not talking to strangers, etcetera, Francis takes off into the carnival with Nathan in tow.

"Wait!" I yell but they don't hear me. I push Daniel forward. "Do not let Nathan out of your sight."

For once Daniel listens and runs after them.

"What do you think's going to happen?" Carter asks.

"I don't know, but I do know Daniel will watch out for Nathan. He always does."

"Trust goes both ways," Carter repeats what Joanie White said.

"I agree, but Francis hasn't earned my trust yet."

"As you haven't earned his."

I turn to fully face my husband. "It doesn't matter if it's Francis or some other ten-year-old boy who just took off with my youngest. I wouldn't trust anyone but Daniel."

Carter doesn't respond to that. Instead, he looks down at the tickets he just bought for the two of us. He sighs. "How about we try to have some fun?"

"Fine." I fall in step beside him. "Did you talk to Francis about breastfeeding?"

"Yes, and he understands it's not something you do. I wish you would've been part of that conversation. He's easy to talk to."

My gaze roams the carnival, bouncing off all the kids and adults, rides, and booths. I spy the three boys standing in line at the tilt-a-whirl. "What about what happened in the grocery store?"

"He feels so bad about that."

"No, he doesn't. You should have seen him. He knew what he was doing."

Carter doesn't respond.

"What, you don't believe me? You should have seen his devious little smirk."

"Devious little smirk? That's a bit much. He doesn't know the parameters yet. He's learning." Carter stops at a stand and buys a cone of glazed pecans. He hands them to me, probably as a peace offering. "Your favorite," he says.

Eating glazed pecans is the last thing I want to do right now. But I take one, holding the cone out for Carter. He selects one as well. I glance over to see the three of them now on the tilt-a-whirl, laughing and screaming.

"Speaking of parameters," I say. "Did you talk to him about Rachelle's ashes and what's appropriate? They're currently residing in the laundry room smack dab in the center of that stupid dog cage."

"Yes, we've decided to have a painting commissioned."

I stop walking. "A painting of what?"

"Of the sunrise. He said his mom liked to watch it while she drank her morning tea."

"Okay, that sounds fine." I start walking again. I eat a pecan. I offer one to Carter and he shakes his head no.

I say, "What about all that medieval torture talk?"

"What about it? There's not a whole lot we can do. Rachelle allowed him to read whatever he wanted to read. They talked about anything and everything. All we can do is keep an open line of communication and answer questions that may come up."

"I'm pretty sure he's the one who shot Boots."

Carter stops walking. "What are you talking about?"

I search the crowd, now spying them at the ring toss. "The cross-stitch he gave Minnie had a bullseye over Boots' eye. The boys were shooting a BB gun the day Boots got injured. I asked Daniel about it, and I know he lied."

"Maybe Daniel shot him."

"What?" I scoff. "You and I both know Daniel's a horrible shot."

Carter looks away. "I'll ask Francis about it. I'm doing the best I can, Tori. I can't force my son to act a certain way or speak differently or tell us more about his life with Rachelle. I'm, *we're*, playing the long game here."

"Are we? I would think if you're 'playing the long game' you'd have signed those adoption papers. Instead, you can't find them."

"Then print off another set," he snaps.

My eyes narrow. "I want you to get *your* son out of *my* son's room as soon as possible. Turn the TV room into a bedroom, build on, I don't care but make it happen."

"Dr. Dixon said—"

"I don't care what Dr. Dixon said!"

A few people pass by, glancing over as we glare at each other.

"What about M&M?" I demand. "Did you ask him about Nathan's guinea pig?"

Carter blinks. His brow knits together. His jaw muscles flex.

"Let me guess—"

"He took M&M downstairs to play with him, but he got away," Carter quietly admits. "He was afraid to tell us."

"Oh, bullshit! Francis didn't even like M&M. He did something to him. I know he did." I throw the pecans away and whirl around to look for the boys. My gaze bounces off the ring toss, the pie-in-the-face booth, the Lego building competition, the funnel cake trolley. "Where are they?"

"They probably went to the contortionist show."

"That's not for another hour." I start walking. I survey the face painting line, the giant Jenga area, the three-legged race. "Where are they?" I pick up my pace.

"God, Tori, calm down. What about the funhouse? Maybe they went in there."

I look at the artic dunking machine, the magic show, the toilet paper toss. I push my way to the front of the line and run into the funhouse. "Nathan! Daniel!" Quickly, I work my way through the maze of distorted mirrors and out the back. "Nathan! Daniel!"

I sprint past the hot chocolate line, the wheel of fortune game, the portable toilet area—

"Mommy!"

I spin around to see Nathan running toward me, crying, with Daniel right behind him and Francis walking further back. Nathan lands solidly against me and I lift him. Loudly, he sobs into my neck.

Carter races around the corner, coming to a stop when he sees us.

"What happened?" I demand when Daniel finally catches up.

He jabs a finger at Francis. "He dragged him into the snake tent."

The furious glower Francis shoots Daniel is brief. I would've missed it if I hadn't been looking at him, but he's quick to switch to remorseful.

"I'm sorry," he says, straightening his bowtie. "I didn't realize Nathan would be that scared."

"You know he's terrified of snakes," I snap. "I know you know that. Don't you pretend otherwise."

With big guiltless blue eyes, Francis looks between me and Carter. "I've heard the best way to face fear is to look it in the eye." He clasps his hands behind his back. "I apologize if I did something wrong."

My arms tighten around Nathan, and I press a kiss to his wet cheek. "It's okay, baby, I'm here. I've got you." He continues to cry.

I stare into Francis' calculating gaze. I am so mad right now I don't know what to say. Holding Nathan, I turn away, pausing to make eye contact with Carter. But he's not looking at me, he's staring at his son with an uneasiness I've never seen before.

Good, maybe this will wake him the hell up.

There is something deeply disturbing about Francis.

43

That night Nathan begs to sleep in the master bedroom and even though I hold him all night, he still wakes with nightmares of snakes attacking him.

The next morning, I leave him tucked in, and I come downstairs to find Carter in the kitchen making breakfast.

"Where'd you sleep?" I ask, and he nods to the L-shaped sofa in front of the fireplace.

I pour coffee. He cracks eggs into a bowl. I sip my coffee. He whisks milk into the eggs.

"I grounded Francis," he says, not looking at me.

"Good."

"He said he's going to apologize to Nathan today." Carter turns the heat on under the skillet. "I'm also going to move Francis into the TV room which means the flat screen will come downstairs. It's not ideal, but it'll get us through until I can build on."

"That's the way it was originally supposed to be with the TV room being Samantha's bedroom," I say.

"I know that. I helped John design this place. Sometimes I think you forget that." Carter places butter in the skillet and it melts to coat the surface.

I sip my coffee. "I don't want Nathan knowing that Francis let M&M out of his home. Emotionally, Nathan's been hit with a lot. First with 'falling' out of the tree. Then losing M&M. Now this snake thing. I find it interesting that Francis was involved with each one."

With a spatula in hand, Carter finally looks at me. "The tree thing was an accident. Francis apologized for that. And it's not his fault M&M got away. I think it's great he brought him downstairs to play."

I huff a laugh. "God, you are so blind."

Carter tosses the spatula into the skillet and shoves it away from the burner. He turns off the heat. "Do you want me and Francis to move out?"

Yes, is the first word to pop into my head, but before I can say anything, Francis treads down the steps.

Carter takes a deep breath and turns away from me to look at his son.

I sip more coffee, watching Carter's "mini-me" quietly cross the great room to where we stand in the kitchen.

"Good morning," he meekly says.

"Good morning," Carter greets him.

I say nothing.

From behind his back, he brings out a pack of cigarettes, a lighter, and several photos of naked women. He lays them on the kitchen island. "I was up in the fort yesterday and found these."

Carter doesn't say a word, he simply slides me a smug look that says *Looks like I'm not the only one with a bad son.*

~

WITH DANIEL GROUNDED for the things Francis found in the fort *and* Francis grounded for the snake incident, things around the house are quiet for the rest of the weekend. Daniel spends it in his room getting caught up on homework and working ahead in each subject. Francis does the same. Nathan stays glued to my side as we help Carter turn the TV room into Francis' bedroom.

To my delight, Nathan doesn't complain about losing Francis as a roommate. But he does ask, "Can Daniel sleep in my room now?"

"No, sweetheart." I kiss the top of his head. "But I'll read you a story and stay with you as long as needed to fall asleep."

"But what if I have more nightmares?" he whines.

"Then I'll be right there to hug you," I promise.

The weekend goes by and neither Francis nor Daniel speaks a word. Sunday night at dinner, they're silent as well.

So is Carter.

It is the quietest our house has ever been.

I look at the two grounded boys. "We've spent the weekend turning the TV room into Francis' bedroom. Each boy now has their own space. All TV will occur down here, that is when the two of you earn the privilege back."

"Yes, ma'am," Daniel mumbles.

"I'm sorry," Francis says to Nathan. "I'm so very sorry. I'll never do anything like that again. I thought it would be good for you to face your fear of snakes. I'm truly sorry. Will you forgive me?"

Nathan looks right at me.

"It's up to you," I say. "He's not asking me that question, he's asking you."

Nathan glances at Carter, but my husband is busy sulking and poking at his macaroni and cheese.

"I guess." Nathan shrugs.

"Thank you." Francis smiles. "I'll be a better big brother I promise."

Nathan sort of smiles back.

The table once again falls silent.

That night I put Nathan to bed. At two in the morning, I tiptoe down the hall to check on him and I find Daniel sleeping with him, his arms wrapped tight, protecting him from bad dreams.

Bad things.

Bad little boys.

44

The next morning, Carter drives the boys down the ridge to catch the bus to school. As I sip the last of my coffee, I study the notes for my morning meeting. A couple of things catch my eye, and I walk into Carter's home office looking for a post-it note.

I find a stack next to the shredder, peel off a couple, and turn. Something sticking out of the claws catches my eye. It's the red legal seal from my office.

I pull the scrap free and study it. I don't remember shredding anything.

Taking the top off, I dig down in. My fingers sift through the paper, and I bring a clump out. It's mostly white and thin with a few thick green chunks mixed in.

Green...

I look further down in the bin, finding more thick green shreds.

Green was the color of the folder that had the adoption papers.

The front door opens, and Carter walks in. At first, he doesn't see me across the great room in his office. He goes about taking his coat off and looping it over a hook. He lowers the heat to the temperature he prefers. He crosses over into the kitchen and begins loading the dishwasher. Turning toward the center island, he glances up.

That's when he sees me kneeling on the floor in his office.

I hold up a wad of shredded white and green. "Are these the adoption papers?"

He flounders for a response.

"Carter, did you shred the adoption papers?"

"Of course not."

I stand up. "Then how did they get shredded?"

"I don't know." He shakes his head. "Maybe I accidentally put them in with a stack of other things."

"You never accidentally do anything when it comes to your office. You're more organized than I am." Carrying a handful, I walk out into the great room. "Maybe this was your way of delaying things."

"Oh my God, Tori, really? You're being paranoid."

"Am I?"

He glares at me. "Okay, you want to have things out. Let's do it. How about we start with your dead husband who you still think you're married to."

"Fuck you."

"Nice language, Tori."

My hands tighten into fists.

"Or how about we talk about the pills you don't think I know you take."

My jaw clamps so tightly I fear I might crack a tooth. But it's the only way I can stop from screaming.

"Or let's chat about losing Samantha because you still haven't told me about that."

My body shakes with uncontrollable fury.

"Or what about the fact you never talk to me. Jesus Christ, Tori, you're like a goddamn vault!"

I give into the scream, throwing the scraps of paper at him. "It's your fault John is dead!"

Carter lurches back as if I punched him in the gut. His face pales.

"You were there," my voice shakes. "You were there on that river. You were his kayaking partner. You were supposed to watch over him. You let him die. You failed. You should have noticed he was in a tricky area. Those rapids took him under. You didn't get to him quick enough." My voice breaks. "It's your fault."

Silence.

I cry.

Carter's face crumbles. "My best friend died in my arms. It was the worst day of my life, Tori."

"You should've known how to save him!"

"I tried. GODDAMMIT, I TRIED!" Grabbing a wine glass from the open dishwasher, he hurls it across the kitchen. It hits the wood-planked wall and shatters.

Loudly, I sob.

But he doesn't come to me. He stomps across the house, flings open the door, then slams it behind him.

∾

THE REST of the day and night my husband and I don't speak to each other. Carter once again sleeps downstairs.

In the morning, I'm putting clothes away in Nathan's room when I overhear him and Daniel in the bathroom.

"Are Mommy and Carter fighting?" Nathan asks.

"Yeah, I think so," Daniel says.

"Did I do something wrong?"

"No," Daniel says. "I'm pretty sure it's about Francis."

Done brushing his teeth, Daniel leaves the bathroom and Francis walks in. He takes a turn at the sink. The two boys don't speak.

Nathan's just about to leave when Francis says, "Daniel's right. They're fighting about me. I think they want to send me back."

"Oh...well, do you want to leave?"

"No, I want to stay. I love being your brother. I am sorry about the snake thing." He pauses. "Will you like me again? I hate that you don't talk to me."

"Okay, I guess I'm done being mad."

"Really?"

"Really," Nathan says, and I hear a smile in his voice.

When I glance out his bedroom door and down the hall, I see the two boys hugging. After turning out the light, they leave the bathroom and go downstairs.

"Do you want me to tell Mommy and Carter that I want you to stay?" Nathan asks.

"Yes, please." Francis takes Nathan's hand.

Despite my feelings for Francis, their exchange still tugs my heart. Nathan is such a kind and forgiving kid.

My cell buzzes with a text.

Picking it up off of Nathan's dresser, I swipe my finger. It's from the Private Investigator.

CHECK YOUR INBOX.

45

With everyone downstairs, I close myself in the master suite and slide my laptop from its soft case. I bring up the email.

Tori,

It's no wonder you couldn't find anything on Rachelle Meade. Her real name is Lindsay Fowler. Please find an article attached.

I pull the article up, noting the date some twenty years ago.

Orphan Lindsay Fowler was 11 years old when 48-year-old Jake Monte approached her outside her foster home in Saratoga Springs, New York. He held a gun to her head and forced her into his car. He transported her to an isolated cabin in the Catskill Mountains where he introduced her to his wife and accomplice. For eight years Lindsay was held in a dog cage. She was repeatedly abused and sexually assaulted, resulting in two sons.

Jake Monte was caught when he showed up at the local hospital with one of his sons who had ingested poison. His erratic behavior led a police officer to question him and eventually reveal the truth. Despite Fowler's claims she was there of her own free will, both Jake Monte and his wife received life sentences. Both committed suicide within one year of their term.

Lindsay Fowler changed her name and relocated; destination unknown. Her two sons born in captivity were taken into custody.

I narrow in on "For eight years Lindsay was held in a dog cage" and my stomach twists.

That poor girl.

I read the article again, this time slower, focusing on, "Despite Fowler's claims she was there of her own free will..."

It reminds me of a Stockholm Syndrome case I studied in college. There was a young woman held captive for nearly a decade. Despite the emotional and physical abuse, she bonded with her captor as a way to survive. She even wept when she was rescued, and he was killed by police.

Rachelle Meade, aka Lindsay Fowler, did what she had to, to survive. She convinced herself she liked what they were doing to her. She pretended so long that she came to believe it herself.

Also attached to the email is a picture of 19-year-old Lindsay Fowler when she was found. Such a pretty girl with long red hair, sweet freckles, and bright eyes. She hooked up with Carter roughly one year later and nine months in came Francis.

I type her captor's name into a search engine, "Jake Monte." A picture pops up of a good-looking man with blonde hair and blue eyes, just like Carter.

No wonder Rachelle picked Carter out at that bar. He reminded her of her captor. She had two boys taken from her. It wouldn't surprise me if she got pregnant on purpose, trying to replace what she had lost.

Somewhere out there, Francis has two half-brothers.

Once again, I read the news article, and this time the first part draws my eyes. *Orphan Lindsay Fowler.* The P.I. did not include anything else. I type, "Lindsay Fowler," into a new tab and get back over sixteen million results.

I send a text to the investigator: ANYTHING ON LINDSAY FOWLER BEFORE THIS ARTICLE? WHY WAS SHE AN ORPHAN?

While I wait for a response, a deep breath leaves my lungs. She was found at 19, still basically a child, and according to the article, relocated soon after. I imagine the horrors Rachelle lived through, repeatedly abused by that couple.

Did she repeat the pattern with Francis?

My phone buzzes with a return text. YES, I WAS ABOUT TO EMAIL YOU A SECOND ARTICLE. LINDSAY'S PARENTS WERE SHOT IN A HOME INVASION. SHE SAW THE WHOLE THING.

My blood freezes in my veins. For the first time since hearing about Rachelle Meade, my heart aches for her.

What a tragic existence. It doesn't make any sense. How can so many horrible things happen to one innocent little girl?

46

T hat afternoon Carter has a meeting, leaving me to after-school activities. It's gymnastics day for Nathan and foot-ball conditioning for Daniel. Francis typically stays with Carter and does homework while they wait on the two others. Even-tually, we need to figure out an after-school activity for Francis.

Something shifted in me this morning after finding out about Rachelle's background. I debated on if I should show it to Carter and Dr. Dixon. In the end, I decided yes. I emailed all the information to Dr. Dixon and cc'd Joanie White, and then I showed the findings to Carter.

He cried, and I held him as I found myself sliding over to his and Francis' side. I wanted both of them—no, all of us—to come through this.

I'd walked downstairs where the boys were in the kitchen eating breakfast, and I had hugged each one of them and told them, "I love you."

Including Francis.

He is all I have been able to think about today. Even now as I sit here outside of school in the pick-up line.

The bell rings, and I straighten up. Kids emerge from school in gossipy clumps. Teachers urge them along to the busses and cars. The air is alive with a different type of chatter.

I spy Francis first. He smiles and waves a little too excitedly, almost giddy. Nathan is second. He looks around, confused at the commotion. Daniel comes third, mirroring Nathan.

The three boys climb in, Daniel in the front with Francis and Nathan in the back.

"What's going on?" I ask.

"Dr. Dixon was arrested," Francis eagerly announces. "They found child pornography in his office."

I gasp.

"What's that?" Nathan asks.

"Naked pictures of kids," Francis answers as he clips his seatbelt on.

Nathan's eyes widen.

"Dr. Dixon was in the locker room yesterday." Daniel looks over at me, sick. "Was he. . . looking at us?"

"Probably," Francis says.

My eyes flick to him in the rearview mirror. He's busy smiling and looking out the window.

Why is he so happy about this? "This has to be a mistake," I mumble. "Dr. Dixon is well thought of in this community."

The crossing guard waves us on, and I pull from the school onto the main road.

Francis puts a piece of gum in his mouth. "I'm glad he's gone."

"Why?" I ask.

"He's nosy. I like Joanie White better."

"But, he gave me a purple pencil for being kind." Nathan's bottom lip quivers. "He wouldn't do that if he was bad."

I take a breath, looking again at Francis in the rearview. He blows a bubble. It pops. He begins humming, *All around the Mulberry Bush, The monkey chased the weasel. The monkey stopped to pull up his sock, Pop! Goes the weasel.*

47

T hat night after dinner, Carter and I sit alone in front of the fireplace, him with a beer and me with wine.

Francis comes down the stairs to stand on the landing. "I read that a teacher gets replaced when they die, retire, or are fired," he says. "According to the internet, child pornography is the number one thing to get a teacher fired. When will Dr. Dixon be fired?"

Carter and I exchange a look.

"We don't know anything," I say.

"If he doesn't get fired, then when will he retire? He's old and old people retire. Right?"

Again, Carter and I exchange a look.

This time Carter replies, "Yes, old people eventually retire."

Francis sighs. "Well, if he doesn't retire or get fired, then I guess dying is the only other alternative."

Carter doesn't look at me. He stays focused on his son. "Dying is not an alternative. Why would you say that?"

"No reason."

He starts to walk back up the stairs, and Carter stops him. "Francis, when I asked you about Boots you said you may have shot him. You didn't know for sure. You can tell us if you accidentally shot him.

Accidents happen, we know that. What's important is that you don't lie. Tell the truth."

"What if it wasn't an accident? What if I shot him on purpose? Would I be in trouble?"

Carter puts his beer down. He takes some long seconds to formulate a response. His voice comes low, almost panicky. "Are you saying you shot Boots on purpose?"

Francis blinks. "Would I be in trouble?"

"Yes, you would."

He smiles. "Then I guess it's good I'm joking."

"Is that the truth?" Carter asks.

"Yep, that's the truth." He skips back up the stairs.

My husband and I are silent for several long seconds. Just this morning I'd rallied behind Francis. I'd been ready to understand him and make this work. In a matter of one single day, I'm back to doubt and uneasiness. I can tell from Carter's disquiet that he's feeling it, too.

Did Francis have something to do with this Dr. Dixon thing? As soon as I think about it, I discount it. How is that even possible?

Boots, though, I'm not so sure.

Carter picks his beer back up. "Dr. Dixon's been around a long time. He's a husband, a father, a grandfather... What the hell?"

"I know."

"Has the school released any information yet?"

"No, but I know the lawyer who handles school union stuff. He said the pictures were stuff you can print right off the internet. Like kids in underwear and naked children on the beach."

"Still." Shaking his head, Carter gets up, walking toward the downstairs bathroom. "I'll be right back."

With a nod, I sip my wine and I stare into the soft glow of the fire. I grew up in this area. Dr. Dixon was a brand-new teacher when I was in elementary school. I was never in his class, but I remember him. I never got a strange vibe.

Which makes this so puzzling.

My thoughts bounce around after that, going from the newly

acquired information on Rachelle back to Dr. Dixon, to cases I'm currently working on.

Yet, as I settle back into the sofa and continue to sip my wine, Francis is once again all I can think of.

Rachelle was kept in a cage. If she repeated that behavior with Francis, why isn't he more scared of the one currently sitting in our laundry room, still with the baby rattle and his mother's ashes? Why does he seem so well-adjusted and unaffected by the living situation he came from?

48

The rest of the week goes by. Though nothing has been officially announced, Dr. Dixon took retirement. His situation will be settled out of court. My union lawyer friend says there's a strong case someone planted the photos in his office.

Francis' response to the situation led me to poke around his bedroom, but I found nothing.

Around the house, things have been weirdly normal. The boys get up and go to school. I head to work. Carter handles things from home. After-school activities occur. Francis signs up for gymnastics. We eat dinner as a family. Homework, bath time, then bed. Nathan's once again sleeping through the night.

But on Sunday afternoon when I step from my bedroom and hear arguing, I pause to listen.

"You're grounded for two weeks. You're not supposed to go to the fort," Francis says.

"Shut up," Daniel snaps. "You don't know what you're talking about."

"I saw you climbing down."

"You did not."

"I did too."

"Yeah, well you tell on me, and I tell on you."

I follow their voices to Daniel's closed bedroom door.

Francis lowers his tone to a hollow level. "You threatening me?"

"Maybe I am," Daniel challenges.

Silence.

Daniel says, "You don't fool me."

"I just want to be brothers."

"Oh, bullshit," Daniel snaps.

Again, silence.

I move closer to listen.

Calmly, Francis replies, "I get it. Brothers fight. Fighting means we care. We love each other."

"I don't love you," Daniel snarls. "I've got a brother and his name is Nathan. I don't need another."

"It hurts my feelings to hear you talk that way," Francis calmly replies.

"God, you are such a freak! Get out of my room."

"Whether you like it or not, I'm part of this family now. They turned the TV room into my bedroom. They love me and want me to be here."

"They don't love you. They didn't even know you existed until a few weeks ago. They have to keep you. They don't have a choice."

Another beat of silence goes by.

"Same goes for you. Carter feels obligated to keep you. That's why he hasn't signed the adoption papers yet."

"I hate you."

"I'm sorry you feel that way. At least Nathan likes me. I think I'll go see what's he's doing."

Daniel lowers his voice to a warning level. "You stay away from Nathan."

"Hm."

"Get out!"

Footsteps shuffle across the floor heading toward the closed door. I move quickly, ducking into the boys' bathroom. I peek out, watching

Francis emerge. He leaves Daniel's door open as he crosses the hall to Nathan's room.

He knocks, then opens the door. "Hi, Little Brother, want to play?"

"Um..."

"What's wrong?"

Nathan hesitates. "I don't want to play Bad Kitty anymore."

"Okay. We'll go outside."

Daniel charges out of his room. "Then I'm going with you."

Francis looks over his shoulder and his lips curl slowly upward. "Why, I think that sounds delightful."

~

FROM THE BANK of windows that front our house, I watch them play. Or rather, Francis and Nathan play as Daniel stands nearby cautiously inspecting their every move.

Carter works out of his office with his door closed for a weekend conference call. As I listen to his muted voice and continue watching, I replay their words.

Yeah, well you tell on me and I tell on you.

Tell on him for what? What does Daniel know about Francis that he's not telling?

They don't love you.

God, you are such a freak.

I hate you.

I've never heard Daniel say such mean things. It embarrasses me, but it alarms me more and makes me think about our conversation a couple of weeks ago with Dr. Dixon and Joanie White. They said children were a good judge of character.

I just want to be brothers.

It hurts my feelings.

Fighting means we care.

Francis responded so calmly, so controlled, even when he said, "Carter feels obligated to keep you."

I don't want to play Bad Kitty anymore.

What the hell kind of game is Bad Kitty?

As I continue watching them, I do some random searches on my phone. "How to handle children who have been abused"; "Long term effects of abuse"; "Child Neglect."

I scroll the feeds on each search. Reading similar advice: make sure the child is safe, communicate openly, provide emotional and spiritual support, maintain honesty, show love but ask permission before touching, establish ongoing counseling, create boundaries as children do respond to authority.

With a glance out to the boys, I close out that window on my phone and pull up another. A link labeled, "How sociopaths are different from psychopaths," catches my eye. I click on it, at first skimming as I did the others. But there's too much of interest. I want a bigger screen.

With one last check on the boys, I walk over to Carter's iPad laying on the couch, and I bring up the link.

People who are sociopathic or psychopathic are those who exhibit the characteristics of antisocial personality disorder, typified by the pervasive disregard of the rights and/or feelings of others.

I pause, typing, "antisocial personality disorder," into the notepad on my phone.

Then I continue reading,

Psychopaths are classified as people with little to no conscience who follow social conventions when it suits their needs. Sociopaths have the limited ability to feel empathy or remorse and react violently when confronted by the consequences of their actions.

Psychopaths pretend to care. Sociopaths make it clear they do not.

Psychopaths display cold-hearted behavior. Sociopaths are prone to fits of rage.

Psychopaths maintain a normal work and family life. Sociopaths cannot.

Psychopaths love people in their own way. Sociopaths have relation-
ships that are shallow and fake.
    Sociopaths recognize they are doing something wrong and rationalize
their behavior.

I pause for a second to type a reminder search, "is it possible to be both?"

People with Antisocial Personality Disorder go to extraordinary lengths to
manipulate, charm, disarm, and frighten to get their way.
    Psychopaths have a history of unstable family life, often going back
generations. Sociopaths are associated with adverse childhood experiences.

That sentence leads to a hyperlink labeled, "Psychopaths are born. Sociopaths are made."

I pause there, backtracking to type in, "Antisocial Personality Disorder," and a list is the first thing to pop up:

- Lie, con, and exploit others
- Can be irritable and aggressive
- Act rashly
- Fight or assault others
- Fail to meet social duties
- No signs of remorse after hurting others

The list continues, but I stop there and bring up the reminder search I had typed in, "Is it possible to be both a psychopath and sociopath?"

I skim the first link, picking out the phrases: *No clinical difference. Often used interchangeably. Depends on the length of behavior. Both are severe cases of antisocial personality disorder.*

With a sigh, I sit back, and I stare at the coffee table as I work things through in my mind. Psychopaths are born. Sociopaths are made.

If that's the case, then Francis would be made not born. Unless what happened to Rachelle factors in. Then Francis was born, not made. Does that make him both, then?

The hairs on my neck shift with a breath that crawls my neck.

In front of me, the fireplace sits ashy with charred wood from last night's fire. Above it, a framed photo of the Tennessee mountains in full spring bloom reflects back a person standing behind me looking over my shoulder at the iPad still in my lap.

Francis lifts his gaze to meet mine in the reflection. "Which one am I? A psychopath or sociopath?"

49

"How long have you been there?" I'd asked, quickly standing and moving away.

"A second," Francis had replied. "Or two."

"I didn't hear you come in."

"Which one am I?" he'd repeated.

"Neither. I was doing stuff for work."

That conversation replays in my head as I sit at dinner idly listening to Carter, Francis, and Nathan talk about gymnastics. Daniel's quiet. I'm quiet.

How long *had* Francis been standing behind me?

I'm not sure, but I am sure he didn't believe me. He knows I wasn't doing work.

Loudly, Carter clears his throat. "I have an announcement." He reaches under his chair and brings out a green folder. He opens it and pulls out a legal document I recognize as the adoption papers. I didn't print off new ones. He must have asked my assistant at work.

Carter looks between Daniel and Nathan. "Any idea what this is?"

Daniel shrugs.

"This says I'm your legal father. All your mom and I have to do now is go in front of the judge, which is just a formality." Carter walks the folder around the table to me, and I fabricate a smile as I take it.

I wish he would've given this to me in private.

Or rather not in front of Francis.

Because if I'm being honest, I'm not entirely sure I want this now.

We exchange a chaste kiss. Nathan cheers. Daniel sneers at Francis as if to say *Carter feels obligated to keep me, huh?*

Francis eyes the folder, watching as I lay it to the side. Something calculating crosses his expression as if he's devising a plan.

No, not a plan. A new plan.

He's the one who shredded the original set. I'm not sure why I didn't think of that until now, but it's true. I know it is.

Francis peels his gaze away from the green folder. He eats a piece of corn bread, taking his time to chew and swallow. I can almost see the wheels turning as he thinks. Formulates. Devises a new strategy.

Delicately, he wipes the corners of his mouth. He places the napkin back into his lap and looks right at me. "If Daddy is adopting Daniel and Carter, that means you're adopting me. Right, Mommy?"

～

THAT NIGHT the boys are in bed. Carter's in the bathroom, and I sit in the corner lounge chair of the master bedroom. I've been here for the past hour pretending to work.

Carter wants to talk about me adopting Francis, and I want to talk about anything but.

The bathroom door opens. I concentrate on my screen.

Carter pauses in the doorway, eyeing me. I know he's debating whether or not to interrupt me.

Heaving a sigh, I rub my temple. If I'm busy enough, and stressed, we won't have to talk about this.

Quietly, he treads over to the gun cabinet. He turns on the interior light, studying it for a second. "Did you open this?"

I shake my head.

He double-checks the key is on top where he usually leaves it before moving over to the king-sized bed. He slides into his side and picks up his phone. He scrolls, eyeing me over the top.

My fingers race over the keys. He's an early-to-bed, early-to-rise type of man. If I wait long enough, he'll tire before me.

A few minutes go by. Carter puts his phone down.

"Did you see the email that Ms. Sally-Anne is sick, and they haven't found a sub driver yet?" he asks.

Quickly, I shake my head.

"That means one of us will have to take the boys to school tomorrow morning. I have that early call. If we need to ask Minnie, we should do that now before it gets too much later."

"I'll take them," I mumble.

"Okay."

I keep typing. He keeps patiently waiting.

"Why are you working so late?" he asks.

"Last minute client," I reply, typing, typing, typing.

"Oh." He slides down in bed, getting comfortable. "Well, we need to talk about you adopting Francis when you're done with that."

I give a distracted nod.

More minutes tick down.

He picks up his phone again, scrolling, trying to stay awake. But eventually, his eyes close, his breaths even, and I stop pretending to work.

Conversation successfully avoided.

For now.

50

The next morning, the house is busy with the usual Monday morning chaos. I overslept because I was "working late." Carter throws together breakfast. The boys run around getting ready for school. Carter disappears into his office to get ready for his early call. We load up into the SUV.

At school, I take my place in the drop-off line. Luckily, Nathan chatters on and on, leaving no room for Francis to ask follow-up questions about adoption. Because, like his father, I know he wants to talk.

Eventually, we reach the drop-off zone and they climb out. It's as I'm about to pull from line and head to work, that a pretty dark-haired woman smiles and waves as she sidesteps a group of girls.

I roll the passenger window down. "Joanie? What are you doing here?"

She reaches a gloved hand in to shake mine. "I'm the new Dr. Dixon!"

"Oh, wow. Congratulations."

"Thanks. I'm thrilled." Her smile grows wider.

"Are you Dr. White then?"

"Soon. By the summer I'll finish my dissertation."

"The school is lucky to have you."

"Thank you. Listen, I've been going through Dr. Dixon's schedule, transferring it to mine. Tomorrow he's scheduled to meet with Francis, which I plan on doing. I'm hoping you and Carter can come in later this week, so we can chat? I'd love to know how things are going."

"Sure, that shouldn't be a problem. Carter will be thrilled to hear you're here."

"Great! I'll send you both a few times and you can pick one."

She moves away from my SUV and on a quick thought, I ask, "I don't suppose there's been anything else on the Dr. Dixon situation? Last I heard he was taking retirement and it was being settled out of court. Something about planted photos?"

"You didn't hear? They found copies of the exact photos from Dixon's office in a girl's notebook."

"What girl?"

"I believe her name is Maia."

∾

THAT NIGHT at dinner I look right at Francis. "Are you excited Joanie White has taken the place of Dr. Dixon?"

"I am. I like her so much. She's pretty. I'm the one who called her and told her Dr. Dixon was a pedophile and got fired. If she wanted his job, she could have it."

Carter stops eating.

"Who's Joanie White?" Nathan asks.

"She's the one who came and got me from the trailer when Mommy died. She's the new Dr. Dixon."

"He didn't get fired," I say. "He was forced to retire." I look at Carter. "They found the evidence in a girl's notebook."

"What girl?" he asks.

"What's evidence?" Nathan says.

"It's proof Dr. Dixon isn't a bad man," I answer.

"I heard it's Maia," Daniel answers Carter's question.

"Correct." I direct my focus on Francis. "Would that be the same Maia you had an issue with?"

"She got suspended over it." Smugness creeps into his expression. I look around the table. No one notices it but me.

"There has to be a mistake," Carter says. "Why would a ten-year-old girl do such a thing?"

Francis cuts into chicken fried steak.

"I don't like Maia," Nathan says. "She's mean. So is Chris."

Francis eats the meat. "Yes, they are a very bad little boy and girl."

~

AT BEDTIME, I linger in Nathan's room.

"What kind of game is Bad Kitty?" I quietly ask.

He looks toward the door.

"It's okay. You can tell me."

"Francis tells me I'm bad and puts me in the cage."

Uneasiness settles in my chest. "Nathan, I don't want you to play that game."

"I don't want to play it either. Can I tell him no?"

"Of course, you can. Promise me you will."

"Okay, I promise." He snuggles under the covers. "Will you read to me now?"

I don't read him the usual one, or even two, but three bedtime stories. I barely hear the words over the cycle of *Bad Kitty* that whirls through my brain.

Nathan is asleep well into story number two, but I keep reading. I read so long that Carter finally tiptoes in.

"You coming to bed?" he whispers.

Reluctantly, I nod.

With one last kiss to Nathan's head, I follow my husband down the hall and into the master suite. After closing the door, I turn to look at him.

He doesn't waste any time. "I'd like to discuss you adopting Francis. It only makes sense. Now that things are legal with Nathan and Daniel, let's make it legal with all three."

"Things aren't legal with Nathan and Daniel, not until we go in front of the judge."

Carter just looks at me.

"Also, I want more information. Now that we know Rachelle's back story, I want more insight into Francis. What all did she do to him, Carter?"

"Why can't you just draw a line and move forward? Why do you keep digging? What exactly are you hoping to find?"

"More. I want all the information I can get. Did you know Francis has been putting Nathan in the cage?"

Carter's shoulders drop. With a heavy sigh, he sinks onto the bed. "Of course, I didn't know that."

"Nathan just told me. It's a game called 'Bad Kitty.'"

A long moment goes by, then he says, "I'll talk to Francis."

If Carter were John, this would be the perfect time to share my research on anti-social personality disorder and sociopath versus psychopath. We would discuss it rationally, analyzing each detail. But Carter will never be John. Just like Francis will never be my son.

"Did you get the email from Joanie White?" I ask. "This 'game' is something we need to tell her."

"Agreed. When do you want to meet with her?"

"As soon as possible," I say.

"Pick a day and time and let me know. I'll make it work." He pushes up from the bed and walks into the bathroom.

The door closes, and a relieved breath leaves my lungs that the adoption discussion is on hold, for now.

I re-open the bedroom door, ready to brew my nightly mug of herbal tea, just as Francis disappears down the hall and into his room.

He was listening to our conversation.

If this was Daniel or Nathan, I would not put up with that behavior. I won't allow it from Francis, either.

I tread down to his open door. He's already tucked in bed,

feigning sleep. A nightlight plugged in beneath his desk casts an amber glow over his floor. I walk to his bed.

He opens his eyes and looks up at me through an innocent blue gaze. "I was in the bathroom," he says as if anticipating my words.

"You weren't listening at our door?"

He blinks. "No, ma'am. Of course not."

I study his guiltless expression.

Liar.

51

L ate the next afternoon I navigate my SUV along the ridge up to our house. The sun glows winter bright, warming the dust of snow that fell along the mountains last night. It'll be dark within two hours. The sun always seems to set quickly in the winter. It's here, and then it's suddenly gone. Unlike summer where the transition from day to night lingers for hours as the sun gradually melts into the horizon.

The last email I read before leaving work came in from Joanie White, confirming our meeting tomorrow morning. I plan on discussing my concerns in full to include anti-social personality disorder. With both Joanie and Carter in the meeting, it will be a safe space. We'll have Joanie's rationale and expert opinion weighing in, or rather softening the blow as Carter comes to realize the depth of his son's issues.

I pull under the house and park. As I open the driver's door, I hear *Mommy!*

The word comes faint and distant, floating on the wind.

I pause. "Nathan?"

"Mommy!" Louder this time, coming from the woods that border the back of our house.

I drop my things and run. "Nathan!"

"MOMMY!" Nathan careens from the trees. "Help!"

"I'm here!" I race to meet him, but he doesn't run into my arms. He turns around and sprints back. "Help, it's Daniel!"

In my long leather coat and dress shoes, I rush after him.

"The trucks," he pants.

"What trucks?"

He scrambles over a downed tree. I nearly fall on my face as I hurtle it. "The logging trucks?"

He nods, increasing his pace.

Fear floods my body. "What happened?"

"He fell," Nathan gasps for air.

"*From the cliff?*"

Nathan nods and my heart contracts. Oh my God.

"And got hit." He wheezes for air.

"BY A TRUCK?" I scream.

We emerge from the trees. Francis is the first person I see, standing at the edge looking twenty feet down to the winding road.

My heels dig in, sending loose rocks and dirt over the edge. I look down and my blood runs cold. Daniel lays face up, his ankle bent at an odd angle. A logging truck sits idling mere feet away with the driver crouched over him and on the phone.

"Daniel!" I scream, choking on his name.

The trucker looks up the cliff. "He's alive," he yells. "I'm on with nine-one-one."

My breaths come heavy with both panic and relief. *He's alive.* I turn to Francis and the look on his face turns my cold blood to ice. He's staring down with a keen curiosity that sickens me.

My jaw clenches. "What. Happened?"

"It was an accident."

52

Dislocated shoulder. Concussion. And a broken ankle, now with three pins in it.

It could be so much worse.

My baby. My firstborn. It was just me, John, and Daniel for seven years. We did everything together. We were there when he said his first word, *hiya*. We were there when he crawled and when he walked. We fed him his first solid food. John and I photographed every moment of his life. We took hundreds of photos. Heck, maybe even a thousand.

And now here he lays asleep, having just come from surgery on his ankle.

My fingers tighten around his. "I'm right here, Daniel."

The door to his hospital room opens and Carter quietly enters with Francis and Nathan. "The doctor said we were free to come in?"

Absently, I nod, not taking my eyes off of Daniel. When he wakes up, I want my face to be the first thing he sees.

Nathan scoots in beside me, and I open my arms. He slides up onto my lap.

"Is he going to be okay?" he whispers.

"Yes," I assure him. "He'll make a full recovery."

Nathan looks at his elevated foot, thick with a cast. "Will that hurt him?"

"He's got lots of pain medication in his system. He won't feel that foot." I kiss Nathan's head. "You're going to have to be a great brother and help him once we get him home."

"I will." Nathan nods. "I promise."

Francis takes the chair on the other side of the bed, and Carter stands beside him. Carter says, "I had a cast on my wrist when I was a teenager. It's going to itch like crazy. But the fun part will be when his friends draw on it and sign it."

Nathan smiles a little. "Maybe I can put a sticker on it."

"Daniel would like that," I say.

"His brain banged against his skull. That's a concussion. I looked it up." Francis cocks his head, studying Daniel's face. "No screen time, rest, and no activity. That's how you treat a concussion. I looked that up to."

"His brain banged his skull?" Nathan whispers.

My free arm tightens around him. "Yes, but he's going to be okay."

Francis taps the sling wrapped around Daniel's arm and it's all I can do not to snap at him, *Back the hell away!*

Daniel moans and stirs then, and gently, I push Nathan off my lap. I stand up. "Daniel, I'm right here."

His lips move. "Mom?"

"Yes, I'm right here." I run my fingers through his dark hair that curls slightly around his ears and neck, just like John's hair.

"So am I," Nathan says.

"Me, too," Carter puts a hand on his knee. "We're all here."

Francis once again touches the sling around his arm. "I'm here, too."

Daniel peels open his eyes and my face is the first thing he sees. I smile, and slowly, he blinks. "You're okay," I softly say. "I'm right here."

His lips move again. "Thirsty," he croaks.

The ice is on the other side of the bed and Francis moves quickly, grabbing the plastic glass and fishing a chip with his fingers. Before I have a chance to intercede, he slips it inside Daniel's mouth. My son's eyes stayed glued on me as he sucks and swallows.

"Better?" I ask.

"More," he rasps.

As if anticipating that response, Francis pushes another inside his mouth. Daniel's still looking at me as he again sucks and swallows.

I smile. "You're going to be okay."

He frowns a little like my face is going in and out of focus. The doctor said that would probably happen. He blinks, looking from me down to Nathan. Nathan grins. Daniel tries to smile back, but his face scrunches in discomfort.

I run fingers through his hair again. "You can close your eyes. Rest. I'll be right here when you wake back up."

His eyes close. His head turns away. Slowly, his eyes open back up and they freeze wide when they land on Francis.

"Hi, Big Brother." Francis straightens his bowtie. "It's nice to see you. Why don't you close your eyes and go back to sleep? We'll all be right here when you wake back up."

~

"I'M GOING to sleep here with Daniel tonight," I tell Carter. "I called Minnie and she's going to watch Nathan. She'll be here to pick him up in a few minutes."

"I'm perfectly capable of watching both boys. Why did you call Minnie?"

"Because...because I thought you said you had an early meeting," I fib. "I was trying to help ease the load." I press my fingers to my temple. "I'm sorry. I'm overwhelmed. It doesn't matter. Minnie's already agreed."

Carter wraps his arms around me. "It's going to be okay."

With a nod, I step away. "I want to get back to Daniel." Over his shoulder, I spy Francis at the nursing station talking to a volunteer. A smile cinches her cheeks and she chuckles at whatever he just said. I turn toward Daniel's room. "I'll see you tomorrow."

Carter and Francis leave. Minnie arrives to pick up Nathan and to give me an overnight bag. A nurse brings a cot in for me, but I stay right beside Daniel's bed, holding his hand.

Somewhere around one in the morning, I drift off and when next I open my eyes, the sun is coming up. I see Daniel staring at me.

"Hi." I smile and my fingers flex around his hand.

"I'm hungry," he says, and I chuckle. That's my son.

A nurse comes in and while she checks on Daniel, I make a quick trip to the bathroom in his private room. When I come back out, Daniel's drinking orange juice and eating graham crackers and a banana. The nurse is gone.

"She brought a banana for you too," he says, eating nearly half of his in one bite.

I press a kiss to his head before taking my banana and sitting carefully on the side of his bed. "This okay?" I ask.

He nods.

For a quiet moment, we eat and share orange juice. The nurse brings me a cup of coffee. Gratefully, I smile. "Thank you."

"The doctor will be here in about an hour," she says, leaving us once again.

"How are you feeling?" I ask him.

He yawns, looking at his foot and then his arm. "I'm okay. A little tender, but I'm not in pain."

"Good." I sip my coffee.

"I take it my foot is broken?"

"It's your ankle. You had to have surgery. You've got three pins."

"Cool."

I laugh.

He holds up his wrapped arm. "What's up with this?"

"It was dislocated, but they worked it back into joint. You've also got a concussion. So, if your vision is a little blurry or your memory is fuzzy, that's why."

He munches a graham cracker. "Guess this means I'm out of football."

"Winter conditioning, yes."

"Bummer."

"You'll be good for the new season, though."

He nods.

I drink more coffee, studying him. "Daniel, do you remember what happened?"

"I went to watch the logging trucks..." A frown line gathers between his brow as he thinks.

"Were you alone?"

"Yeah, after what happened the last time, I wanted to go by myself."

"What happened last time?"

"I went with Francis, but he pushed a big rock over the cliff and it caused a truck to wreck." His frown deepens. "He said it was an accident, but I don't think it was."

I have no idea what Daniel is talking about, but I file that away for now. I'm more interested in what happened yesterday afternoon. How did my son, who has watched the logging trucks nearly every week for the past two years, fall twenty feet to land in front of a semi?

"How did you fall, Daniel?"

He looks away, and I can see him digging in his brain, pushing puzzle pieces around. I wait patiently. Several long seconds go by, then he says, "I was arguing with Francis. I told him to stay out of Nathan's room. I caught him standing over Nathan's bed just staring at him. It creeped me out. Francis was doing that stupid innocent smirk thing that he does. It pissed me off. I got right up in his face. That's when he shoved me...and that's the last thing I remember."

53

That afternoon, I stand in the hospital corridor, looking right at Francis. Nathan is beside me, holding my hand. Carter comes up behind Francis. Good, he needs to hear this.

"Francis, what happened at the cliff?" I ask.

"It was an accident," he says. "I tripped and knocked into him." He looks down at Nathan. "Right, Little Brother?"

Nathan steps closer to me.

I'm not doing this lying thing. "Daniel said you two were arguing. He got in your face, and you pushed him. You pushed him so hard he went over the cliff."

Francis looks between me and Carter. "It was an accident."

A nurse passes by, and I nod down to Nathan. "Is there someone who can watch my son for just a few minutes?"

"Sure." She smiles at Nathan and holds out her hand. "I was just about to grab a popsicle. You like popsicles?"

Eagerly, he nods as he takes her hand and follows her.

When they're down the hall and out of hearing range, I look back at Francis. "Why have you been watching Nathan sleep?"

"Tori," Carter mumbles, but I don't look at him. I keep my gaze fastened on his son.

Francis shrugs, but he doesn't deny it.

"Daniel said that's what you were arguing about."

Francis nods.

"It is not okay to be in Nathan's room. You have your own room." I lean down. "Do you understand me?"

"Yes."

Carter puts an arm around him.

"It was an accident," Francis repeats, looking up at his father.

"An accident." I straighten up. "Like with the big rock you 'accidentally' pushed over and caused a truck to wreck?"

"What are you talking about?" Carter asks.

"I don't know, Francis." Both my brows go up. "What *am* I talking about?"

"I'm sorry. It was when I first got here. I went with Daniel to see the trucks. I was sitting near the edge and when I stood up, a big rock rolled over and down. One of the trucks braked to a stop and some of the logs rolled free. Nobody was hurt. I was so scared. I asked Daniel not to tell on me." Francis looks up at Carter, all guiltless and helpless. "I'm sorry."

Carter sighs. "Francis, that's a big deal. You can't keep stuff like that from us. Do you understand?"

"I do." Francis looks at me. "I'm sorry, Mommy."

It's all I can do not to snarl at that word.

Minnie steps from Daniel's room, pausing in the hall when she sees the three of us in a standoff. Nathan returns with the nurse, his lips bright purple from the popsicle he's currently licking.

Minnie says, "Why don't I take them to the cafeteria?"

"Thank you." I nod.

The nurse lets go of Nathan's hand and Francis immediately takes it. I hate that he does that. I watch Minnie walk with them down and around a corner.

I turn to Carter. "If I find Francis standing over Nathan's bed, I'm going to lose it."

"I'm sure—"

"You need to think hard about all the 'accidents' that have happened since Francis arrived. Because until he came into our lives, we lived a pretty great day-to-day, accident-free existence."

54

"She scares me sometimes,'" Joanie says. "Those were his exact words."

"Oh, that's a bunch of bullshit," I reply before snapping my mouth shut. This meeting is not going well and looking impatient is the last thing I need to do. But my God, can't she see that Francis is manipulating her?

Our meeting with Joanie White got pushed due to Daniel's accident. After another night in the hospital, we got him home and settled in his room. The weekend went by uneventfully. I tended to Daniel, who is, as expected, bored out of his mind. There are only so many video games, TV, books, and board games you can play. Both of my sons are outdoor boys. I can already tell this will be a long recovery for all of us.

Carter kept Francis busy for the weekend. Minnie volunteered to take Nathan, but I declined. Nathan's about the only one who seems to amuse Daniel right now.

I came to this Monday morning meeting ready to detail my concerns, *yet again*, but I've been bombarded.

Francis doesn't feel like you're bonding with him.

Francis doesn't think you want him.

Francis thinks you like Daniel and Nathan better than him.

Francis thinks...

Francis thinks...

Francis thinks...

I am about to scream.

"Listen, there's something you need to know." Joanie pauses, looking first at me, then Carter. "I did an activity with Francis. I gave him a selection of dolls and told him I'd love to see a scene from his prior life. Sometimes it's easier for a child to show than to tell. He selected three dolls: a mother, a young boy, and a baby. He then proceeded to draw a picture of a cage and he placed the mother doll inside while the boy doll stood outside, looking in. He said, 'You're a very bad kitty.'"

I draw in a breath. "He did that with Nathan."

"I'm not sure I understand." Carter shifts forward. "I assumed Rachelle had done things to Francis. Are you saying it's the other way around?"

"We see this in people who've experienced traumatic situations like Rachelle. She hated herself and believed others should hate her too. Rachelle was addicted to the abuse she sustained from the couple who kidnapped her. Probably without meaning to, she inadvertently taught Francis how to continue the abuse. It helped her feel worthy and loved. She put herself in the cage. It made her feel safe. She not only allowed Francis to be cruel to her but wanted it, even needed it, possibly encouraged it. Frankly, I'm not sure she knew anything else."

My stomach twists into a knot that sickens me.

Carter says, "You said he selected three dolls. What about the baby?"

A look of concern etches Joanie's brow. "He placed the baby inside of a bathtub. I asked if the baby was him and he said, her name is Petra."

"P-Petra?" I glance at Carter. "He told us Petra was his mother's pet."

Joanie thinks about that a moment. "Petra could have been a pet.

Or Rachelle may have had another baby. There are different ways it can be interpreted. It's better not to press him. He'll tell us about Petra when he's ready." She looks between us. "Did he ever show you those Polaroid photos?"

"No," I answer. "He may have thrown them away or shredded them." Because I certainly looked for them in his things.

"What about the notebook I told him to keep?" Carter asks. "He never brings it home. Have you seen it?"

"Not yet, but he's close to showing me." Joanie uncrosses, then recrosses her legs. "It annoyed him that Dr. Dixon constantly asked about it. I'm giving Francis the space to bring it to me on his own. I strongly reside in the clinical framework that complex trauma and adverse experiences, particularly in early childhood, result in complicated mental health." Joanie smiles a little. "We had a big breakthrough, but we've only just scratched the surface. In the meantime, let's talk strategy. Francis needs to be involved in social activities with other children. This will teach him conflict resolution and emotional management skills."

"We've got him in gymnastics," Carter's quick to say.

"Good." Joanie nods. "Counseling is a must, which he gets with me. Let's also think about a mentoring program. I understand he has a great relationship with Nathan. How about I look into tutoring opportunities with younger children."

"That sounds great!" Carter looks at me.

"I wouldn't say he has a 'great' relationship with Nathan. To me it's more like Nathan is his pet. He's always holding his hand, leading him around." It's weird, I want to say but don't. "Daniel also found him in Nathan's room, watching him sleep."

"He's trying to feel safe and loved," Joanie says. "I understand he's a lot to deal with." She hands us each a brochure. "I'd like to recommend Parent Management Training. Research has found that warmth and affection, reasonable discipline, and an authoritative parenting style have positive outcomes for children like Francis. He's different. He's unique. But he will come out of this. Hang in there."

She looks between us. "Both of you."

She and Carter continue talking. I want to ask about all the "accidents" that have happened since he arrived, but the longer they talk, the more fixated I become on Joanie's words.

She not only allowed Francis to be cruel to her but wanted it, even needed it, possibly encouraged it.

PART IV

Carter

55

"They'll believe me over you," Daniels says.

"You sure about that?"

"Don't mess with me, Francis. You'll regret it."

"Really?" Francis chuckles. "I'm not the one with a cast now, am I?"

"Boys." I step into Daniel's room to see him sitting at his desk and Francis standing in front of him. "What's going on?"

Francis turns away. "Nothing, Daddy."

I look at Daniel, but he keeps glaring at Francis. "Get out of my room. Now."

I have an older brother, and we fought pretty much every single day. We said horrible things to each other. But we also loved each other fiercely. My parents interceded all the time, breaking up our fights. They'd send us each to our rooms and in the morning, we were back to normal.

Until the next time we fought.

I follow my parents' lead now, sending Francis to his room and closing Daniel's door.

In the master suite, I find Tori sitting in the corner lounge chair staring at printed pages.

Usually, I'd prod her.

What's wrong?

How are you doing?

What are you thinking?

But none of those come out. Instead, I avoid her by going to the bathroom and shutting the door.

Yesterday morning, she left the meeting with Joanie without a word. I thought we'd talk afterward, but Tori walked right past me and out of the school. She climbed into her SUV and pulled away.

That afternoon Francis and Nathan got off the bus. As usual, I picked them up and drove them up the ridge to our house. Tori hadn't been far behind. She spent the rest of the day and evening hovering over Daniel and Nathan, leaving me and Francis to ourselves.

Today I showed up after school, as I always do, to pick the boys up for activities. However only Francis climbed into my Jeep.

"Where's Nathan?" I had asked.

"Mommy got him and took him home."

Silently, I transported Francis to gymnastics. I sat in the bleachers staring at my phone, oscillating between calling Tori, or not.

In the end, I did not and two hours later when I arrived back here at the house, I was half expecting her to be packing her bags to leave me.

But, she wasn't.

Instead, she once again spent the evening hovering over Daniel and Nathan.

Now here we are, me in the bathroom and her out there.

I stare at myself in the mirror. What would I do if the situation was reversed? I'd be all in, I know I would. I'd go to parenting classes. I'd do whatever was recommended to see one of her sons through anything. Yet she's not willing to do the same.

She's leaving me. I know it.

With a deep breath, I open the door.

Tori looks up.

I want to conjure the endless patience and compassion I have for her, but instead, anger fires through me. It's not fair that I took on raising her sons, yet she won't put any effort into helping me with mine.

I flick off the light, but I don't cross over to her. I stand right where I am.

Looking back to the papers, she reads, "Antisocial Personality Disorder in children is characterized by aggression, deceitfulness, defiance. Symptoms—"

"Stop it."

She doesn't miss a beat. "Symptoms lead to animal and human abuse, lying, violating rules, and destruction of property. Some signs—"

"I said, stop it."

"Some signs are lack of empathy, disregard of authority, using charm to manipulate, and arrogance. Risk factors—"

"This isn't fair, Tori."

"Risk factors include genetics, poor parenting, and tumultuous home life." She looks up at me. "What's not fair?"

"All of this. I've more than stepped up for you and the boys. I've happily stepped up. But you? You've dropped the ball."

She makes no expression. She doesn't care. "Do you know your son needs help?"

"Yes," I snap. "Yes, I know he needs help. Yes, he checks some of those boxes, but some he doesn't. For that matter, Daniel and Nathan check a box or two from your *precious* list."

Still, Tori seems unfazed. Calmly, she slides from the lounge chair. She crosses over to the door and opens it to find an empty hall. Closing the door, she turns to me.

She holds up the papers. "Rachelle Meade, aka Lindsay Fowler, was eight when someone broke into her childhood home and killed her parents. She was eleven when she was abducted, repeatedly abused, and held captive for eight years, resulting in two children that were taken from her. Fast forward one year and she picked you that night. Whether you realize it or not, you resembled the madman who twisted her head and made her think she loved him. She picked you and along came Francis."

Though I know all of this, the words still punch into me.

"And now here you are, *we* are, left to deal with all that violence wrapped up in one ten-year-old boy." She shakes her head. "She allowed that boy, *your* son, to be mean to her. How far did she let things escalate? Do you not wonder that? Do you not—"

My hand slices through the air. "Enough!" I tread across the master suite and come to a stop in front of her. "This has to stop. What happened with drawing a line and stepping over? What are you trying to prove?"

"If you have to ask me that..." Tori looks away from me, shaking her head again. "This isn't working. Wake the hell up and realize it. Francis needs more help than any of us can give him, including Miss White. I want him out of this house. He needs to be institutionalized, or...give him back to the system."

My jaw drops. "What the hell, Tori? Give him back? Who are you right now?"

She stares me hard in the eyes. Then she delivers the line I've been dreading. The words shatter my anger and destroy my heart. "It's either me and my boys or Francis. Pick."

56

The next morning, I lay wide awake in bed, listening to Tori breathe deeply with the type of sleep she gets from taking one of her pills.

Except, I didn't see her take one.

There is something wrong with him, Carter.

You need to think hard about all the "accidents" that have happened since Francis arrived.

He needs to be institutionalized.

My son is different, I know that. But if there was some extreme underlying dangerous and alarming issue requiring an institution, wouldn't Dr. Dixon or Joanie White have detected it?

Yes, they would have. That's their job.

It's either me and my boys or Francis. Pick.

What the hell am I going to do?

With a quiet sigh, I push the covers back and swing my legs over. The gun cabinet casts a yellow glow over the room, and I use the soft light to navigate by.

After a quick trip to the bathroom, I silently take the steps down. Halfway to the bottom, I hear rustling coming from the kitchen.

On the landing I spy Daniel propped up on his crutches, going through the spice cabinet. He opens a container and dumps the contents into a paper bag.

What the...? "Daniel, what are you doing?"

He doesn't look at me. He gets another spice container, opens it, and dumps it as well.

"Daniel." I come off the landing and cross through the great room. I grab his arm. "Daniel."

He pulls away, gets another, and dumps it out.

"Daniel." I try again, but he ignores me, emptying yet another.

He works fast, almost frantically. His pace increases as he fists another and pours it out.

Pepper. Tumeric. Basil. Paprika. Salt. Dry mustard. He's emptying them all. I don't know what to do. Something is wrong.

I try one last time to stop him and he snaps, "Let me do this."

I take a step back.

Francis comes down the stairs, pausing at the landing to watch the sun make its first appearance.

Daniel continues working.

After a few seconds, Francis walks over to the kitchen island and climbs up on a stool. Calmly he watches Daniel, seemingly unfazed by the situation.

I look between them.

Done with the spice cabinet, Daniel moves over to the refrigerator. He opens the door, grabs all the fresh herbs from the bottom bin, and tosses them on top of the dried ones. He studies the contents of the refrigerator, and apparently appeased, he closes the door.

Carefully, he scrutinizes the kitchen. He opens the canister of sugar and dumps it down the garbage disposal. He runs water, watching it grind and disintegrate.

That's when he sees my son sitting on the other side of the island watching him.

Francis smiles. Daniel glares as he turns off the disposal. He snatches up the paper bag and hobbles it over to the door that leads to the wrap-around deck. He opens it and limps out into the cold dressed only in his pajama bottoms and a tee.

I watch through the windows as he slowly makes his way around to the charcoal grill. He opens the lid and places the paper bag down in the briquette area.

"What is going on?" I turn back to Francis.

"Why are you asking me? He's the one acting weird."

Through the windows, Daniel's now squirting lighter fluid over the bag. I rush out the door and around to the grill. "Daniel, stop this."

He puts the fluid down and flicks a lighter. It flares, then fizzles. He flicks it again.

"Daniel!" I grab it. "What is going on?"

"Burn this now. I mean it, Carter. Burn this now."

"Okay. Okay." I hold the lighter to the bag, flick it a few times, and it finally ignites.

Daniel backs up a step. Flames flick to life, sending out black smoke and a pungent smell, like the wrong kind of incense has been mixed. It burns my nose.

Daniel doesn't move. He watches the paper and spices burn until ashes are the only thing left. Only then, does he turn away.

My hand latches onto one of his crutches. "Daniel," I quietly say.

Finally, he looks at me and I see something in his gaze I've never seen before.

Terror.

"You can talk to me," I say. "Please. What's wrong?"

He opens his mouth and his bottom lip quivers with something unsaid.

"Daddy?" Francis rounds the corner of the porch to where we stand. "Can we eat breakfast now? I'm hungry."

I keep my focus on Daniel, but he turns away, mumbling, "Just leave me alone."

57

B reakfast comes and goes. Daniel and Nathan are eerily quiet. Francis isn't, though. He talks quickly, moving from one topic to the next. "I think it would be so fun if we all played hooky one day from school and work. There's a kid in my class who does that every month with his family. Last month they went to the aquarium in Chattanooga."

"Ms. Sally-Anne has a birthday coming up." He forks up a bite of pancake. "I think I'll cross-stitch a school bus for her. Or maybe not. Something, though."

He chews, swallows. "Joanie White told me I'm going to be mentoring a couple of first graders. That'll be neat. That's just a grade above you, Nathan."

"Maia comes back next week from her suspension." He drinks orange juice. "I hope she's learned her lesson."

He slides from the island stool and carries his plate to the sink. "By the way, Daddy, I'm ready to commission that painting with Mommy's ashes. I have something special in mind beyond what we already talked about."

"But I'll tell you about my special idea later. It's a secret." Francis rinses his plate, then loads it in the dishwasher. "No, not a secret. More like a surprise." He turns and looks at Nathan. "Are you done, Little Brother?"

Nathan's barely eaten anything. But he quickly nods and scrambles down from the stool.

Francis holds his hand out and Nathan hurriedly takes it. "Come along. Let's get you in your coat and gloves. We're going to play outside."

"Nathan," Daniel speaks.

They stop.

"You don't have to go with Francis if you don't want to."

"Don't be silly." Francis waves him off. His hand tightens around Nathan's. "You want to come with me, don't you?"

Nathan looks right at me, and I see the mirror image of Daniel's face from earlier.

Terror.

He's always holding his hand, leading him around. To me it's more like Nathan is his pet.

Tori's right. I can't believe I didn't see that until now.

I walk over and disengage their hands. "Francis, you go play outside. Nathan needs to finish his breakfast." I don't give my son a chance to argue. I take his coat from the hook, hand it to him, and open the door. "Stay where I can see you."

Francis smiles sweetly. "Of course, Daddy."

Closing the door behind him, I turn right as Tori slowly crosses the great room. She presses a hand to her head. "My head is killing me."

"You slept hard last night," I tell her.

"It doesn't feel like it. I feel like I could sleep another twelve hours. Maybe I'm getting sick." She looks between the boys, confused. "Why are you here? It's a school day."

"Inservice," Daniel tells her.

"Oh." She trudges around the island to the coffee and pours some into her *Dear Mom, At least you don't have ugly children* mug. "I should probably call in sick. There's no way I can work today." She sips. "Where's Francis?"

"Outside." I nod for Nathan to take his seat again. "You need to eat."

Thankfully, he digs in.

I look right at Daniel. "Do you want to tell your mom about this morning or shall I?"

He shrugs. "You can."

"I came down early to find Daniel emptying every spice we have into a paper bag. He took it out to the grill and lit it on fire. He won't tell me why." Leaning back against the counter, I fold my arms. "Maybe you will now that your mom's here."

Daniel picks at his pancakes.

Tori looks at me. I keep staring at Daniel.

"Daniel?" she prompts. "Why would you do that?"

"Because...because I was afraid there was poison in them."

"Why would you think that?" Tori asks.

"Francis knows all about herbs and flowers and stuff from his mom, I guess, and books. Whatever. Like he mentioned something about oleander and jimsonweed and that people die from eating them. He said it would be easy to mix things into spices and take out a whole family." Daniel pushes his plate away. "I got paranoid and thought he'd done something. It was stupid. I'm sorry. I let him get inside my head."

"You have nothing to apologize for." Tori puts her mug down and goes around the island to hug Daniel.

Nathan nudges his plate away too. "I'm not eating that."

Tori looks at me over the top of Daniel's head.

"I'll handle it." I push away from the counter and on my way out the door, I grab my jacket.

As I zip up, I take the stairs down under the house. Other than our vehicles, the parking area sits empty. "Francis?" I call out with no answer.

I pace a few yards into the woods that border the back of our home. "Francis?" I once again call, with no answer.

He doesn't usually go to the fort. That's more Daniel's thing. But I walk the gravel drive down, finding the fort empty.

Again, I call out, "Francis?" And again, nothing.

I backtrack my steps up the drive toward the house. As I walk the last hill, I see Tori in her white robe racing across the porch. She flies down the exterior stairs and takes off down the valley.

"Nooo!" She screams and the high pitch wail ricochets through me.

I run after her. "Tori!"

But she doesn't look back. Her arms and legs pump.

I round the front of the house, following her, and as I peak the valley, I see it. I would've already seen it if I'd simply walked the porch.

Francis stands hunched over the graves with mounds of dirt surrounding him. He wedges a shovel into the ground, pushes it in with his shoe, and levers up another clump of frosty grass and frozen earth.

The world moves to slow motion as I watch the next few seconds play out.

Tori reaches him first. She shoves him hard and he falls back onto the dug-up ground. She grabs the shovel and slings it aside. Francis scrambles to his feet and she hauls off and slaps him solidly across the face. He once again gets back up and she grabs both of his upper arms and shakes him hard. She's crying hysterically by the time I finally reach them.

My heart pounds. "Tori, let him go."

She does, once again shoving him away. She falls to her knees next to the dug-up graves and sobbing, she pushes the dirt back into the holes Francis created.

I don't know what to do. I turn to my son to find him sitting cross-legged, watching her with a dark and shrewd gaze that unsettles me.

"Why would you do that?" I demand.

"The painting we talked about." He looks up at me with eyes that suddenly become clear and innocent. "I thought it would be nice for all of their ashes to be in it as a family portrait. I told you I had some-thing special in mind. This is it."

Tori collapses, holding the clumps of dirt in her arms. She sobs loudly. I try to console her, but she shoves me away, just like she shoved Francis.

"Leave me alone," she cries. "Just leave me alone."

58

An hour later, I'm packing a suitcase when Tori walks into the master bedroom. She pauses when she sees what I'm doing.

Dirt covers her robe, her face, and her exposed arms and legs. Streaks trail her cheeks where she's been crying. Despite her tragic appearance, her shoulders ease when she sees what I'm doing.

"You're leaving," she breathes the words, and all I hear is the relief in her voice.

"Yes, with Francis." My son just dug up two graves. What he did was beyond wrong.

Yet, I've spent the past hour trying to justify it and see it from his point of view. I want to say that he thought he was doing something nice by including all of the ashes in the painting, but that's not true.

Francis knows the graves are off-limits.

The calm and calculating way he sat there and watched Tori tells me everything. He wanted to push her buttons and see how she would respond.

I'm angry, but I'm more ashamed at how much I've let Francis get away with. I have no idea what I'm going to do with him, but I'm hoping Joanie White can advise me.

"Where are you going?" Tori asks, not moving from the doorway.

"I'm not sure, but I do know we won't be here. I'll book a hotel and then figure it out from there." I zip up my suitcase and slide it from the bed onto the floor.

Silently, I study Tori, and the more I do, the more guilt eats away at my insides. "I'm sorry," I quietly say.

She opens her mouth to respond when Nathan steps into the room. His voice is low. "A policeman just pulled up."

59

D own in the great room, Daniel and Nathan sit side-by-side on the L-shaped sofa. Daniel's got his broken ankle propped up on the coffee table and his arm around Nathan. Francis is curled up on the floor in the corner, next to my office, cradling his arm. I don't know why he's sitting over there. He's never sat there before.

And why does he look so scared?

A policewoman hovers near them, protecting.

Tori sits on an island stool with me standing beside her. She's still dressed in her robe and covered in dirt. It makes her look crazy.

A policeman stands in front of us. He surveys Tori's eyes. "Ma'am, are you high?"

"What? No. Why would you ask me that?"

"You look like you had quite the bender last night."

"She didn't sleep well," I say.

"She takes pills," Francis quietly speaks from the corner.

I whirl around to glare at him. The woman cop shifts closer like I'm going to attack him.

"Sometimes, yes," Tori says. "I have prescription medication for anxiety and insomnia. But I didn't take anything last night."

The cop makes a note. "If we were to do a drug test, would you come up clean?"

She bristles. "I know my rights. You can't drug test me."

"Yes, you're a lawyer," the cop says. "Want to tell me why you're covered in dirt?"

"This is all a big misunderstanding," I say.

"Your son called nine-one-one for a reason." The cop gives me a disciplinary look. "Now, let me do my job. What happened here this morning?"

Tori unclenches her jaw. "Francis dug up my husband and daughter's graves. They're buried right out front on the slope of the valley. I was, *am*, understandably upset."

"We were supposed to do a painting with all the ashes," Francis says. "I'm sorry I misunderstood." Once again, he cradles his arm.

The woman cop kneels down in front of him. "Can I see your arm?"

He nods, and gently, she pushes up his sleeve. I draw in a shocked breath, as does Tori.

What the hell?

His upper arm is covered in deep red and purple marks. "It's not the first time she's touched me." He lifts his shirt to show days-old blue and yellow marks on his back.

My jaw drops. I look at Tori, but she doesn't return my look. She slides from the stool to her feet. "He's lying."

"Ma'am, sit back down."

Nathan starts crying and Daniel's arm tightens around him. With tears in his own eyes, he looks at me, but I can barely form a thought. "Th-there has to be a mistake. I-I would know if she touched him."

Wouldn't I?

Of course, I would.

"Carter, I did not do that." Tori takes my hand. "This is a misunderstanding."

"Ma'am, sit back down."

Nathan's cries become louder.

The woman cop looks at Daniel. "How did you break your ankle?"

The question takes him off guard and he looks at Tori. "I-I—"

"They got in an argument," I say. "Fran—"

"I found this in her journal," my son interrupts, presenting a ripped page that he slides from his back pocket.

The woman cop takes it.

Tori steps forward. "That's private."

"Ma'am, sit back down!"

60

(Tori's Journal)

This morning I made love to Carter and as usual, I pretended he was John. It's the only way I can orgasm. I don't think I'll ever not blame him for John's death. Just like I'll always blame myself for Samantha's.

But I depend on Carter. I can't be a mom to Nathan and Daniel without him. It's the only reason why I married him. I needed a partner to help raise my boys.

Though if I could rewind the clock, I would. Because of Francis.

I don't like him. At all. From day one I knew something was off about him. I've tried. I have. There was even a tiny bit of time where I felt we bonded, but it was a blip in the bigger span of weeks gone by.

He's too damaged. Rachelle allowed him to become a monster. Yet, Carter can't see it. Everyone says to support and have patience with Francis, but I don't want to.

I've been sneaking pills again. It's the only way I can control my nerves. If I'm being honest, it's the only way I can control my urges. I want to strangle Francis.

I hate the very sight of him.

61

The female cop escorted Tori upstairs and waited while she showered and dressed. The male cop stayed downstairs with us. I didn't know if I should console Nathan and Daniel, who sat crying and scared on the sofa, or go to Francis, who cowered on the floor in the corner.

I ended up staying at the kitchen island, my gaze bouncing from the cop, to Tori's boys, to my son, and back to the cop.

My brain spun.

I didn't know what to do. This was Tori's area. She was the lawyer in the family.

Lawyer. We needed a lawyer.

I also needed to take Francis to the ER. Or did the cop do that? I didn't know.

I got my answer when the male cop said, "Is there anyone who can watch these two while you take your son to the emergency room?"

Yes, Minnie.

She promptly answered my text and came up the ridge to our home. She hugged me first, barely even looked at Francis, and then went straight to Daniel and Nathan.

They didn't handcuff Tori, but they did put her in the back of the squad car. Thankfully, they allowed her to kiss Daniel and Nathan goodbye.

Francis and I left the house, trailed by the cop car. They followed us to the Emergency Room and waited until Child Protective Services arrived. Then they took Tori away.

In the ER the doctor took pictures of Francis' bruises, sent him for x-rays, and gave him a full physical exam. Thankfully, nothing was broken.

Child Protective Services spoke with Francis first, then me. I don't know what they asked him, but I'm assuming it's the same type of questions Joanie White asked when she first removed Francis from Rachelle's home.

- When was the last time you ate?
- When was the last time you had a bath?
- How do your parents react when you get hurt?
- Who stays with you when your parents leave the house?
- Do you have injuries? How did you get them?
- Do your parents hurt you on purpose?
- Are you scared of making your parents angry?
- What happens when they get upset?
- Who is your favorite person in the family?
- Do you ever want to hurt yourself?

I tried to recall all the questions Joanie said she asked, but my brain was in a million places. More than anything, I wanted to know how Francis answered.

A lawyer arrived, telling me he was a colleague of Tori's.

Minnie called to check in.

The hours ticked by.

And now here I stand in the examination room next to Francis who sits on the table dressed back in his regular clothes. He's sucking on a lollipop, his legs swinging back and forth like he hasn't spent the past ten hours being poked and prodded, both emotionally and physically.

Despite this whole horrible day, my stomach still growls. I haven't eaten anything since pancakes this morning and it's nearing eight at night.

I can't stop thinking about that page torn from Tori's journal, now in police possession.

...as usual, I pretended he was John. It's the only way I can orgasm.

"Daddy?"

I don't look at him. "What?"

"Daniel told me that you said you'd do anything for him."

I nod.

"Would you do anything for me?"

"Mm," I murmur.

"Is that a yes?"

My response comes clipped. "Yes."

Holding the lollipop, he straightens his bowtie. "Would you kill for me?"

62

I don't answer Francis' question.

The doctor interrupts us to release him. Silently, I drive us home. Francis talks the whole way like he's just woken from a good night's sleep.

When we pull up under the house, I turn to him. "Tell me the truth, how did you get all those bruises?"

"I'll tell you, but you have to promise to keep my secret."

"I promise."

He leans in, whispering, "I gave them to myself."

"D-did you tell anyone that at the hospital?"

"No. I told them Mommy gave them to me. She doesn't like me. Now she's gone, and we can be a family. Just you, me, and my brothers." Francis opens the passenger door and jumps out. He energetically takes the steps up.

I follow at a slower, dazed pace.

In the house, Minnie's already put Nathan and Daniel to bed. She takes one look at my face. "Everything okay?"

I shake my head.

Francis slides onto an island stool. "I'm hungry. Will you make me something?"

"Sure," she hesitantly says, eyeing me.

"You got this?" I ask, and she nods.

With heavy feet, I trudge up to the master suite. Francis' babbling voice is the last thing I hear as I close the door.

Physical and emotional exhaustion punch into me and I lay face-first across the bed. I don't care if Francis goes to bed. I don't care if Minnie stays or goes home. I simply don't care.

I close my eyes and I sleep.

~

WHEN I AWAKE, only a couple of hours have gone by. I move to get under the covers and my gaze lands on Tori's mug, still with the herbal tea bag dangling over the side from the previous evening. Her words come back to me. *My head is killing me.*

I'm not sure what compels me, but I sit up and grab the mug. I pick the tea bag up and sniff it. It smells like a mixture of ginger and cinnamon.

He knows all about herbs and flowers and stuff from his mom, I guess, and books.

...something about oleander and jimsonweed and that people die from eating them.

...it would be easy to mix things into spices and take out a whole family.

I'm across the room and out the door in seconds. I pause at the top of the steps, looking down to see a dark stairwell illuminated only by the nightlight at the bottom near the landing.

Still, I go halfway down and peek over the great room, finding it empty with Minnie gone home.

Back up the steps and down the hall I go, checking on Daniel first. He's sleeping soundly, covered by his light blue comforter. Quietly, I cross over and stand near his bed, listening to his breaths. They sound normal and heavy with a tiny snore every few exhales.

I move across the hall to Nathan's door, sitting slightly ajar. He, too, sleeps soundly, covered by two blankets—one stitched with soccer balls and another with cartoon characters. He lays on his stomach and I watch his back rise and fall, like Daniel, a normal rhythm.

A sigh of relief comes from me.

I turn, ready to check on Francis when I see him sitting cross-legged in the corner where M&M's home used to be.

"Hello, Daddy."

"Wh-what are you doing there?"

"Watching Nathan sleep. Why, what do you think I'm doing?"

My thoughts freeze in place, as does my body.

I stare at my son's face, glowing on one side by the red desk lamp that Nathan left on, or Francis turned on to see.

Pushing to his feet, he walks over to where I stand, and he slides his soft hand into mine. "Come along, Daddy. Let's let Little Brother sleep."

63

I lay awake the rest of the night with my door wide open. Every thirty minutes I check, finding all three boys asleep in their beds.

Eventually, I just sit in the doorway, so I can watch the hall and their rooms.

But, nothing happens.

At five in the morning, I go downstairs. In the laundry room sits the dog cage with nothing inside. Where did he put Rachelle's ashes and that baby rattle?

I take a few moments to look around but can't find them.

Locating Tori's jar of herbal tea bags, I dump them all out and examine them. They look untouched, but it would be easy to pry the staple open and add something into each bag.

I don't know anything about herbs, but I do know there are plenty of dangerous and strong ones out there—apparently, oleander and jimsonweed being two. I put all the teabags in a Ziplock, and on second thought, I put them right back. I don't want anything to seem off. Instead, I take the one from Tori's mug, wrap it in plastic, and slide it into my pocket.

That's when I remember the sugar Daniel dumped down the sink.

Tori uses sugar in her tea. I open the empty canister, finding a tiny bit stuck to the bottom. I scrape that into a baggie too.

In my office, I go to power up the computer and find it already ready. I never leave my computer on. I always shut it down.

Plus, it's password protected.

I type in my password, and the screen appears normal. I launch the internet and click on browser history. Carefully, I scroll the links going back weeks and weeks. Everything matches up to the sites I visited.

Wait. I never searched for: "What does it take to get a teacher fired?" and "Pictures of Naked Children."

I select the latter, highlighting the link. Pages of images scroll: children running nude on the beach, children in underwear, full-frontal of children in third world countries, and various others.

These are the photos found in Dr. Dixon's office.

I check the search date and it lines up with everything that happened at school.

I'm the one who called her and told her Dr. Dixon was a pedophile and got fired. If she wanted his job, she could have it.

Son of a bitch.

I type in, "Is oleander dangerous to humans?" and I read, *Oleander remains toxic when dry. A single leaf can be lethal to a child and make an adult severely ill.*

"Dangers of Jimsonweed," I type in after that.

Side effects include dry mouth, dilated pupils, blurred vision, hallucinations, and confusion. Severe toxicity has been associated with coma and seizures.

I pull up the information on the investigator that Tori used, and I send her a quick message: *Do you have access to a lab? Can we meet first thing?*

An email in my inbox catches my attention. It came in last night from Tori's lawyer.

Carter,

Tori is being released tomorrow morning at 9:00. She is allowed to see her boys with supervision. She'll be staying at an extended stay hotel. I'll forward the information on that.

It's a good thing you signed those adoption papers as you'll maintain guardianship until a judge makes a ruling. She'll likely be required to take parenting and substance abuse classes.

We plan on contesting this allegation. I'll call you today when I know more.

Minnie's not up yet, but I still text: I'M KEEPING NATHAN AND DANIEL HOME. THEY'RE ALLOWED TO SEE TORI TODAY. ARE YOU ABLE TO TAKE THEM?

Then I send an email to Joanie White. *We need to speak. It's urgent.*

I do a Google search on institutionalizing children. My gaze scans the first page, picking out phrases like, "There is no basis for a parent to consent to involuntary hospitalization"; "Desperate parents abandon mentally ill daughter, so child welfare will take over"; "A licensed doctor must make the recommendation."

That means I need to find a child psychiatrist.

I do a quick search and jot down a few names, all within an hour of here.

My email dings with a message from the investigator to meet at Tori's office at 8:00 a.m.

I send her a quick reply and my eye catches on a saved search that Tori did on my iPad. The cloud backed it up to my laptop.

How sociopaths are different from psychopaths.

I clink on the link and begin reading pages of research. Sure, Tori shared some of this with me, but at the time I didn't want to hear it.

Now, I do.

The minutes roll from five to six in the morning. Everyone will be up soon.

I keep reading, also keeping one eye on the stairwell for movement. Because somewhere between my son digging up graves and my wife getting hauled off by the cops, I've changed my mind about Francis.

Tori is right, there is something really wrong with him.

64

Daniel hobbles downstairs with Nathan right behind him. Thirty days ago, Daniel would've been complaining about Nathan hovering, but now they're glued to each other.

And Francis is the reason why.

He's terrorized them.

"Daniel." I motion him over.

Gently, he pushes Nathan toward the kitchen before coming to stand at the office door.

I look beyond him, making sure my son isn't coming down the stairs.

I keep my voice low. "Have you seen Francis using my computer?"

He glances over his shoulder.

"It's okay, I'm keeping watch."

"Yes," he whispers like he's afraid to be caught talking to me.

"Why didn't you tell me?"

He doesn't answer.

"Because you're afraid of Francis?"

He nods.

"Do you use my computer?" I ask next.

"No, never."

"Do you know my password?"

He shakes his head.

"How did Francis get it?"

"He said he watched you type it in." He lowers his voice even more. "He bragged about it."

Francis probably stood right there at the door, and I didn't even realize it. A month ago, my son had never watched TV or operated a computer. Now he's online and doing searches for pictures that framed Dr. Dixon for being a pedophile and Maia for planting the photos.

Once again, I check to make sure the stairwell is clear. "Do you remember those Polaroids he kept hidden in his sewing box?"

Daniel nods.

"Have you seen them?"

"No."

"What about the striped notebook that he carries around at school? Have you ever seen inside it?"

Daniel shakes his head.

I hear the upstairs shower go on, and I stand up. "Let's get Nathan. I want to talk to both of you before Francis comes down."

65

Seconds later, Nathan and Daniel sit beside each other on the L-shaped sofa. I look between them, and warmth soothes my soul. I love these two kids so much. "Today Minnie is going to take you to see Tori. You're not going to school. You're going to spend as much time as possible with your mom."

Nathan's big brown eyes grow heavy with tears.

"Did she really make those bruises on Francis?" Daniel mutters.

"Of course, she did," Francis announces, skipping down the stairs. Upstairs, I hear the shower still running. "Your mom is a very bad woman. She deserves to be in jail."

"Francis!" I lunge to my feet. "That is enough."

He puts on the worst fake-sorry expression I've ever seen.

"You're right." He straightens his bowtie. "I shouldn't have said that. I apologize."

"Why is the shower still running if you're dressed and ready for school?"

"Oh, is it?"

My jaw tightens. "Go turn it off, now. Don't come back down until I tell you. I want to talk privately with Daniel and Nathan."

With a shrug, he retraces his steps.

I wait until I hear the shower go off before kneeling in front of them. I lower my voice because I know Francis is listening at the top of the stairs. "This is all a big mistake. We've got a fabulous lawyer who is going to figure this out."

"Is Mommy going to jail?" Nathan whispers.

"No." I make sure he sees how much I mean that. I lean in, tugging them both close. Quietly, I say, "I want you to tell Tori and her lawyer everything you know about Francis. *Everything*."

Sitting back, I look them both in the face. I want them to know how serious I am. *Okay?* I mouth. *I won't be mad.*

They nod.

Minnie knocks on our door. Through the glass panels, I catch her eye and wave her in.

"Francis?" I say, more than yell.

He instantaneously appears, lightly treading the steps down.

Minnie gives him a cursory smile as she crosses over to Nathan and Daniel. I don't know if Tori's been talking to Minnie about Francis, or if Nathan and Daniel have, but I have not. Other than what happened yesterday I'm not sure how much Minnie knows.

She doesn't show Francis the kindness she shows the other two, though. That has to come from somewhere because Minnie is the most loving and giving person who I have the privilege to call a friend.

"Why don't you get yourself together," she says. "I'll make breakfast."

"Thanks."

She jumps right in, making scrambled eggs and toasting English muffins.

Fifteen minutes later I rejoin everyone to find Nathan and Daniel picking at their food. Meanwhile, Francis has cleared his plate as if our whole world hasn't been upended because of him.

"Do I get to stay home from school, too?" he asks. "Nathan and Daniel do."

"No."

"Hm," is all he says.

I look at his empty plate. "Go brush your teeth. I'll take you to the bus."

Thankfully, he does just that.

"Do you want anything to eat?" Minnie asks, handing me a to-go mug of black coffee.

"No." I check the time. "Tori is getting released at 9:00. As soon as I know what extended stay she's going to, I'll text you."

"I'll take them right over," she assures me.

"Thank you." I give Daniel and Nathan hugs as Francis comes back down.

He puts on his coat and gloves and we load up in the Jeep. After I drop him at the bus stop, I drive straight into town where I meet the investigator at Tori's office.

She's already here, sitting in her truck with the engine running.

I walk up to the driver's window, and she rolls it down. I've never met the firm's investigator before, but Tori's mentioned her several times. Her name is Shelby. She drives a black truck, has black hair, and wears a black leather jacket. This woman matches that description.

Still, I ask, "Shelby?"

She nods. "What do you got?"

I hand her the two Ziplocks, one with the used tea bag and the other with the sugar. "I need to know if you find anything odd."

"Like?"

"Like oleander or jimsonweed or anything else that shouldn't be in a tea bag or sugar. The quicker the better."

Shelby takes the zipped bags, gives me a nod, and drives off.

A text comes in from the lawyer with the extended-stay hotel information. I forward it directly to Minnie. As soon as she leaves the house I am going to search the place. I plan on turning our home upside down. I want to find those Polaroids because I know Francis didn't throw them away. He's hidden them somewhere and I intend on finding them.

I climb back into my Jeep right as my phone rings. It's Joanie White.

"Joanie," I say. "There is a lot going on. Yesterday Francis dug up our family graves. He gave himself bruises and told the cops that Tori did it to him. She was taken into custody. He has terrorized Daniel and Nathan. A few hours ago, I found evidence on my computer that Francis framed Dr. Dixon. I'm also pretty damn confident he poisoned Tori. Last night I found him sitting in Nathan's room watching him sleep. It was creepy. He also purposefully—"

"Carter."

I stop talking. "What?"

"Yesterday during the district in-service day, Mrs. Espy, Francis' teacher, was cleaning out the kids' cubbies. Francis' notebook, the one he journals in, fell open. She flipped through it." Joanie pauses. "It's bad."

66

"It's important to maintain a routine," Joanie had said. "We don't want Francis to feel threatened. Let him finish out his morning in class. I'll have him come to my office after lunch. The authorities will be here by then. They'll take him into custody. You'll need to be here..."

She continued giving me instructions, but I could barely focus. The passages she read to me from his notebook spiraled through my head and down to my gut, churning it with nausea.

ENTRY #1
I simply pushed, and Nathan fell so effortlessly from the fort.

ENTRY #2
I fed M&M New Mommy's earrings. He ate them! Then I shoved him in a pillowcase and held it closed. He fought back, squealing. It only took 3 minutes and 6 seconds. I clocked it. I hate that thing. I liked hurting it.

ENTRY #3
Chris clutched his throat. His eyeballs bulged. He stopped breathing. His lips turned blue, just like Old Mommy's lips. Who would've thought his

celery allergy would be such an effective way to deal with him? Now what to do about Maia...

ENTRY #4

I wish I could've seen Minnie's face when she opened her present. She should thank me for shooting Boots, given that he's much more behaved now.

ENTRY #5

New Mommy searched my things. She doesn't think I know. Jokes on her. I moved the Polaroids.

ENTRY #6

Two in one. I got Maia back and also got rid of Dr. Dixon. I can't wait to see Joanie White again!

ENTRY #7

Daniel required more exertion than Nathan. I had to push hard, which was good because his landing was so much more satisfying, especially when the logging truck almost hit him. Too bad the logs didn't fall off like last time. That would've been epic! On the upside, I now have a place to hide the Polaroids. That is until Daniel can climb again.

ENTRY #8

"People with Antisocial Personality Disorder go to extraordinary lengths to manipulate, charm, disarm, and frighten to get their way." Yesterday, I read that on New Mommy's computer. I still want to know if I'm a psychopath or sociopath.

ENTRY #9

Poisoning spices? Daniel's so gullible. I mixed Old Mommy's ashes in weeks ago. I love sitting down for dinner, knowing they're all tasting her.

ENTRY #10

I like Joanie White. She believes everything I say. Stupid woman.

67

My Jeep eats up the gravel as I barrel past Minnie's and up the ridge to the fort. I know where the Polaroids are.

By now, Minnie has taken Nathan and Daniel to see Tori. I dial her number, but it goes to voicemail. "Minnie, please call me at your first opportunity."

A call to our lawyer comes next. It too goes to voicemail. I leave a message.

I start to call Tori before remembering her phone is still in the master bedroom. She didn't take it with her when the cops came.

A glance at my dash clock tells me I only have a few minutes to spare, and then I have to be present at school for when my son is taken into custody by the authorities.

Jesus Christ. I can't believe I just thought those words.

I park at the base of the tree where the fort is, and I make quick work of scaling the planks nailed into the trunk. I shimmy through the narrow cut-out and up into the triangular-shaped space. I crawl over to the corner shelves where Daniel keeps things.

On the bottom sits a metal box where he hid the cigarettes. I try to open it and find it locked. It's an old-fashioned key lock. I whack it a few times against the wood floor and it pops open. Several things tumble out.

The first is a twisted silver ring I recognize from Tori's jewelry box. She never wears it. I think she said her grandmother gave it to her.

Next, I find a swatch of green-flowered fabric. I'm reminded of the photo in Francis' scrapbook of Rachelle. She wore a green flowered dress. Pinned to it is a snack-sized baggie with her ashes inside.

The third item belongs to Daniel. It's a silver dollar he keeps in a box in his closet. John gave it to him.

Next is a small plastic dinosaur from Nathan's collection.

After that is a 50 mm collectible bullet. Which means Francis has been in my gun cabinet.

The last item is the small wooden baby rattle that he kept in the dog cage. A tiny engraving catches my attention. When I first saw this rattle, I looked at it closely, thinking it was Francis'. Now I read the fresh engraving: *Petra*.

Petra was not Rachelle's pet. Francis had a little sister.

I place those items aside. With a rubber band around them, I find the Polaroids wedged in the bottom of the tin box.

The top one is a photo of Francis cradled on Rachelle's lap, breastfeeding. He looks about eight and with her arm extended out, it's evident she took the photo. She's smiling sweetly. It reminds me of the smile she gave me that night I met her at the bar.

The next photo is one of her breastfeeding a baby who must be Petra. Francis has jabbed holes in Petra's face.

I thumb through to the next picture, finding a large dog cage with Rachelle inside. She's dressed in thin pajamas, calmly staring out. On that one, Francis wrote BAD KITTY.

The fourth photo shows Rachelle sleeping. No, not sleeping. She's dead. He took a photo of her dead body with the floor heater that killed her in the background. Around the heater, he drew a heart with a red marker. Paperclipped to the photo is another of a closed-door with a towel stuffed under it. On that one, he drew a smiley face. I check the date and time stamp on each. Francis rigged that heater, stuffed a towel under the door so Rachelle would suffocate in her sleep, then took a picture of her dead body.

My gut churns with nausea.

I don't want to, but I make myself look at the last one. It's Petra in a bathtub covered in water as Francis holds her under.

My son drowned his little sister and killed his mother.

"No." I shake my head. "No."

My throat seizes.

My body heats.

My stomach roils.

Tears burn my eyes.

Lurching forward, I throw up.

~

TAKING EVERYTHING WITH ME, I climb down from the fort.

My phone rings as I put the Jeep in gear. It's Shelby, the investigator.

"We found traces of a common household pesticide in both the tea bag and the sugar. It's easy enough to mask, especially if you mix it with a sweetener."

Tori uses sugar. "Get the results to Tori and her lawyer. Now."

"Sure thing."

We hang up as I drive the rest of the ridge down, once again passing by Minnie's house. I pull onto the highway and navigate through the first part of town. As I come to a stop at a red light, my phone rings again. This time it's Joanie White.

I say, "I'm on my way. I found the Polaro—"

"He's not here."

"What do you mean he's not there?"

"I just called down to Mrs. Espy's room to ask for him, and she said he never came to school today."

Someone behind me honks, and my foot hits the gas. I lunge through the light and jerk my Jeep over into a gas station. "And you're just now realizing this?"

"It's been busy around here. I'm sorry. She left a message for me. I didn't get it until just now. Carter, I'm sorry. I—"

"WHERE THE HELL IS HE?" I yell.

"I don't know."

"This morning I drove him to the bus stop. Where did he go from there?"

"Did you actually see him get on the bus?"

"Shit. I left him to wait with the other kids. Just like I do every morning. Shit. Shit. Shit." I hang up on Joanie and dial his bus driver, Ms. Sally-Anne.

"Hello?"

"This is Carter Grady. Did Francis ride the bus this morning?"

"Oh, I just love your son, Mr. Grady."

"Did. He. Ride. The. Bus?"

"No."

I hang up.

Another call comes in. It's Tori's lawyer.

"I don't have time," I snap, jerking my Jeep into gear. "Francis is—"

"Where are Minnie and the kids?"

My foot slams the brake. "What do you mean where are Minnie and the kids?"

"I'm here at the hotel with Tori and the caseworker. They never showed."

68

D ialing Minnie's number, I race the highway back toward our home.

Like before, it goes to voicemail.

Gravel spits under my tires as I swerve onto our road. At the bottom of the ridge, I jump from my Jeep and run over to Minnie's house. I bang on the door. "Minnie? Nathan? Daniel?"

Nothing.

Grabbing her spare key, I let myself in and run from room to room. Other than Boots hissing at me as I sprint past him, no one is here.

I check her garage to find her Subaru gone.

Back to my Jeep, and I race up the ridge.

I take the last bend and our house comes into view with Minnie's Subaru underneath.

Relief surges through me, followed immediately by dread.

After parking behind her car, I climb out of my vehicle, and I stand for a second, listening. Other than the wind rustling the winter trees, I hear nothing.

I take the steps three at a time up, and I see Minnie the moment I open the door. The cage has been moved from the laundry room to the living room. She lays inside of it with blood pooling underneath her. With wide eyes, she stares straight at me.

My heart stops. *No.*

She blinks. Her chest lifts with a breath. Oh, thank God.

A lock holds the cage together. I recognize that lock. It's from my toolbox in the shed.

Coagulated blood mats the right side of her head and coats her temple down to her cheek. Francis must have hit her, but where is all that blood coming from?

I take a step toward her, now realizing she's been shot—the shoulder I think, or the arm. She puts a shaky finger over her lips. *Sh.* She points upward. *He's got a gun*, she mouths.

"Here kitty, kitty, kitty," Francis calls out, his voice trailing down.

Our knife block sits on the kitchen island. Quickly, I move, sliding one free and tucking it behind my back.

The sound of feet trails the stairs, one soft and one a hesitant hobble.

"I know you're here, Daddy," Francis calls out.

Daniel appears first, his face a mask of forced bravery. Our gazes connect. I search for anything in his eyes that might tell me where Nathan is.

Behind Daniel, my son holds a gun to his head. It's my Ruger revolver.

I focus on staying calm. "Francis, son, what is going on? Why are you doing this?"

He sings, "Rock-a-bye baby on the treetop. When the wind blows the cradle will rock." He pushes Daniel from the landing, gripping his shoulder and keeping the gun pressed to his head.

I didn't show Francis how to load or use any of my guns. I did show him how to use the BB shooter. He has skill and aim. He's already shot Minnie, and I don't doubt for a second that he'll do it again.

"I saw you up in the fort," he says. "I'd like my pictures back, please."

"And your trophies, too?"

A smile creeps across his face. He likes that word trophy.

"Okay," I say. "You can have them. They're down in the Jeep."

"You are a very bad Daddy to steal them."

"Francis, *son*, you need help. Mrs. Espy and Joanie White found your notebook at school. I found the Polaroids. I know what you did to Rachelle and Petra."

"Mommy loved her more than me." His eyes narrow. "I told her it made me angry. She didn't believe me."

I nod to Minnie. "Let her out. Put the gun down. Please, I want to help you."

For a second, I think he's going to comply, but then his lips twitch in amusement. "Oh, now, why would I let her out? She was a very bad kitty. She tried to take the gun from me."

"Where is Nathan?" I ask.

Francis sings, "When the bough breaks, the cradle will fall. Down will come baby, cradle and all."

I stop breathing.

"Nathan is busy." Francis shrugs.

"He gagged and tied him to his bed," Daniel says.

I start to breathe again. Nathan's alive.

"I told you not to speak unless I gave you permission."

Daniel freezes.

Francis pulls the trigger.

69

M y heart rolls over in my chest.

My son tisks. "Oh, well, I guess that wasn't the chamber with the remaining bullet." He cocks it, once again pressing it to Daniel's head.

Minnie cries. "That's the second time he's done that since shooting me."

That revolver holds five bullets. There are only two shots left.

"Now, why don't you put the knife back, Daddy. That is what you're hiding, right?"

Blood thumps in every part of my body as I slide it onto the counter and hold my hands up. "What do you want?"

"I don't want to be locked away. That's what you plan to do with me, right? Old Mommy threatened that too after Petra. But I think it would be epic if we all died together. That leaves New Mommy with all her grief. Poor, poor New Mommy. She'll have so many graves to keep her company."

Beyond the windows, the winter sun tucks behind a cloud. The glass reflects back, giving me a clear shot straight up the steps to where Nathan stands.

He got free.

I keep my attention focused on my son, praying that Nathan climbs from a window, shimmies down a tree, and runs for help.

"It doesn't have to be one or the other," I say. "You're only ten. You'll get the help you need. Francis, I know you've got a lot going on inside of you. Rachelle—"

"I used to love Old Mommy. Until I didn't."

"Why did you stop loving her?"

Nathan moves down the stairs and my mind screams, *No, go back the other way!*

A gentle look crosses Francis' face. "It was just me and her forever. We were soul mates. That's what she said. But then she stopped liking me. She said I was meaner than she wanted. She wouldn't talk to me after Petra drowned. She loved her more than me. Mommy said she was her Little Pet. She used to call *me* her Little Pet. It made me mad."

Nathan shifts to another step, and it's all I can do not to yell at him to run the other way.

"Tell me about Petra," I say.

His face hardens. "What about her? I hated her. She cried all the time."

"Where's her body?"

"I don't know. Mommy buried her in the woods. She wouldn't let me come."

I nod my understanding when everything in me sickens with the repulsiveness of the situation. I imagine Rachelle got pregnant with Petra as she did Francis—on purpose with a random stranger.

"You have two older brothers," I say. "Did you know that?"

"You're lying."

"I'm not. Rachelle had two sons before you were ever born. I don't know where they are, but we can find them. Would you like that? Would you like to know your brothers?"

He doesn't answer, but something shifts in his expression going from smug and calculating to cautious and inquisitive. What I'm saying matters.

Nathan quietly takes one more step down.

"Why didn't she keep my brothers?" Francis asks.

"She wanted to, but the police wouldn't let her."

"Because she was a bad kitty?"

"No, not at all. Because she was very young and not emotionally stable."

Francis is quiet, and I visualize his mind circling around the things I've said. I'm not sure if he knows Rachelle's back story or not. If it were any other ten-year-old kid, there's no way I'd divulge what I know. But Francis is certainly not any other ten-year-old kid.

Another step for Nathan, and I now see what he holds in his hand. I pray he doesn't move. I'm getting through to my son.

"Rachelle was abducted at a young age. The couple who took her did very bad things to her. They kept her captive for many years. It made her into a confused woman. That's why she raised you the way she did."

He frowns. "What do you mean she was abducted? She told me Papa Jake raised her. She loved Papa Jake. I don't understand."

Again, if it were any other ten-year-old boy. "Jake Monte was the man who kidnapped her."

Francis shakes his head. "No, she loved him. She told me she did."

"She was confused."

Nathan slowly moves. Things are about to go from bad to extremely worse.

Francis looks at Daniel, then Minnie, before bringing his conflicted gaze back to mine. "If you're my daddy, who is the daddy of my two brothers?"

"Jake Monte. He wasn't a nice man. He should've never taken your mom."

"So...so she was raped? My brothers came from rape?"

I hate that he knows the word rape at such a young age. "Yes."

His face transitions, instantly going from confusion to full-on rage. Shit. He takes the gun off Daniel and points it at me. Anger fires through his eyes. "Did you rape her?"

The question startles me. "No. Absolutely not."

"P-put it down," Nathan says.

All eyes swerve up to where he crouches on the steps holding Daniel's BB gun pointed at Francis.

My son laughs, now back in his smug and calculating control mode.

Daniel ducks and rams his casted foot back into Francis' leg. He howls in pain. Nathan shoots the BB gun and Francis takes a pellet in the cheek. With a scream, he swerves the gun toward Nathan right as Daniel lunges. The two of them fall to the landing. I race across the floor, desperately looking for the revolver.

They tug at it, back and forth and back again.

"Stay there!" I yell at Nathan.

Daniel gets control of the gun right as Francis shoves him away and lunges up the stairs toward Nathan.

"No!" Daniel screams.

He points the revolver and time suspends as he pulls the trigger.

But, nothing happens. The chamber is empty. That's four.

Laughing, Francis drags a crying and screaming Nathan up the steps.

I grab the gun from Daniel, and I race up just as Francis pulls Nathan into the master bedroom. He shuts and locks the door. I kick it. Kick it. And kick it again. It splinters open, and I race inside to see Francis standing near the gun cabinet. He holds a combat knife to Nathan's neck. He tossed the BB shooter to the side.

Nathan lets out a small sob like he's afraid to make noise. "Daddy, please help me."

It's the first time he's ever called me Daddy.

Francis repositions the blade and it cuts into Nathan's neck.

I lift the revolver and sight it, focusing on my son's face. "Let Nathan go."

An expert tear gathers in Francis' eye. He looks right at me. "Daddy, don't shoot me. I love you."

"Let Nathan go."

"I can't."

"Yes, you can. And you will."

A fresh trickle of blood wets Nathan's neck. He cries.

I stay focused on my son's face. One tear skillfully trails his cheek. He sniffs. But behind all the fake emotion, I see the real monster inside. He's not letting Nathan go.

As if he realizes what I'm seeing, Francis smirks.

I pull the trigger.

That's five.

EPILOGUE

Five years have gone by since I shot and killed Francis. Tori and I are no longer married, but I'm very much part of their lives.

I live in my own place on the ridge. Nathan and Daniel come and go from my house, Minnie's, and theirs.

I often stand on my porch looking out over the valley and wondering if I would do those last few seconds over again. Would I kill my son to save everyone else?

Yes, without a doubt.

Do I question the rest of it? Of course.

I've been in therapy for the past five years, and this is what I've come to accept: I wanted so desperately to have a child of my own that I couldn't see beyond my son's lies and deceit. If I would have realized the level of help he needed sooner, Francis would likely be alive today. I'm not naïve enough to say he would be well and whole, but he would be somewhere safe, making strides toward being a functioning and whole young man.

I drove myself insane with the what-if scenarios. What if I would've searched for those Polaroids sooner? What if I would've hired an investigator right from the start? What if I would've listened to Tori? What if I would've insisted on reading Francis' notebook?

What if...

What if...

What if...

I can't rewind the clock, though. I can only move forward. Which is what I focus on every single day.

"Dad!" Daniel calls, waving. He's seventeen now and looks exactly like John. "You coming or what?"

"Coming!" I close and lock up, joining Daniel to walk the valley up to Tori's house. "What are your plans for the winter formal? Did you ask Winifred?"

Amusement bubbles through his eyes. "I caved and did one of those over-the-top things."

"Don't tell me you did a flash mob."

He groans. "Close to it."

"Aw, don't be embarrassed. Winifred will remember that forever."

"I know I won't be forgetting it any time soon." Daniel tucks his bare hands in his jacket pockets. "Hey, did I tell you we got a new assistant coach?"

"You did. His name is Billy, right?"

"Yeah. He's going to be at the carnival. I want you to meet him."

We walk a few more minutes, talking about Daniel's college applications. He's looking to play football but also major in engineering. John would be proud.

We pass his and Samantha's graves, and I note fresh flowers, signaling Tori was recently here. I often think about that page torn from her journal and it still hurts to know she thought of John so much while married to me. It's something we've talked about in detail. Tori's opened up to me over the years, and I'm at peace with where we are in our friendship. We've come to realize that we rushed into a romantic relationship, both looking to replace the love we shared for John.

We understand that now and accept it.

One day I might find the type of love John and Tori shared, but

I'm in no hurry. I'm okay either way. I'm fifty now and happy, surrounded by those I care for.

Ten-year-old Nathan stands on the deck watching us through binoculars. I make a face at him and he laughs. He disappears inside the house and comes out the other side with Tori trailing him down the exterior steps.

She smiles when we catch up to them. "Hey, you."

"Hey back." She recently grew her dark bangs out and now sports a cute shoulder-length bob. I like it.

I climb into the passenger side of her new SUV and the boys slide into the back.

At the bottom of the ridge, we pick up Minnie.

As we drive into town for the winter carnival, I listen to Minnie chatter on and on with Nathan about the proper way to rappel.

Tori and I share a smile.

Yes, I like my life. Things are good.

Vehicles pack the high school football field. We find a place near the rear of the sectioned-off parking area. The afternoon transitions to evening and the carnival's lights flick on. Music fills the air as does the scent of fried food and sweet treats.

We take our place in line to buy tickets.

"Dr. White!" Nathan calls out.

Smiling, Joanie approaches, holding hands with her wife. She married Laura Harrison, who runs a local plumbing business. She's a good woman. I've worked with her on a few construction projects. They got married last year in an outdoor Spring ceremony that we all attended.

Joanie sweeps a friendly gaze over all of us. "How's my favorite family doing tonight?"

"Good," Tori says. "You getting settled into your new place?"

"Yes, we love it so much." Joanie looks at me. "We were hoping to see you tonight. What's your schedule looking like? We're looking to remodel and build on."

"I'm booked solid for the next three—"

"There he is." Daniel nudges me. "Coach Billy!"

I glance beyond the line of people to see a tall man weaving through the crowd. He hears Daniel and waves. As Coach Billy gets closer, I see that he's young, probably early twenties. He wears a baseball cap and a jean jacket.

He sidesteps a couple of teenage girls and reaches us.

"Coach Billy," Daniel says. "This is my dad, Carter Grady."

Billy takes his cap off to reveal short red hair. He looks me straight on through clear blue, unfriendly eyes. Holding out his hand, he says, "Carter," as if he already knows me.

But I don't shake his hand. I don't move at all. I know exactly who this is. Based on his greeting, he knows who I am as well.

I'm the man who killed his youngest brother.

BOOKS BY S. E. GREEN

Sister Sister

Ambition can be a bitch.

The Family

Be careful what you wish for...

The Lady Next Door

How well do you know your neighbor?

Killers Among

Lane swore never to be like her late mother. But now she too is a serial killer.

Monster

When the police need to crawl inside the mind of a monster, they call Caroline.

Vanquished

A secret island. A sadistic society. And the woman who defies all odds to bring it down.

Mother May I

Meet Nora: Flawless. Enigmatic. Conniving. Ruthless.

ABOUT THE AUTHOR

S. E. Green is the award-winning, best-selling author of young adult and adult fiction. She grew up in Tennessee where she dreaded all things reading and writing. She didn't read her first book for enjoyment until she was twenty-five. After that, she was hooked! When she's not writing, she loves traveling and hanging out with a rogue armadillo that frequents her coastal Florida home.

Made in the USA
Middletown, DE
13 February 2024

49673387R00154